Resonance 3.3

He wanted relief
He found control

By Simon S. Steel

Resonance 3.3

Copyright © 2025 by Simon S. Steel

Acknowledgements

My deepest gratitude goes to those who inspire me to write boldly, without apology.

To my close friends who encouraged me to take this leap into the erotic and the explicit — your laughter, your curiosity, and your honesty kept me going when the pages felt too daring.

To the many readers of my earlier work — thank you for your messages, your feedback, and for letting me know that there is always an audience hungry for more.

And finally, to you, holding this book in your hands: thank you for stepping through the door with me. Without your willingness to explore, these pages would remain empty.

Prologue – Resonance 3.3

Roland hadn't bought the machine for sex. He'd bought it for his aching joints, for the stiffness in his shoulders that no pill ever seemed to touch. But the scalar unit had become a hobby too — late nights with dials, tuning through bands of numbers, curious about what each vibration did to his body.

That night, Sam was with him. His neighbour, his friend. thirty-two, quick smile, short dark hair, and the kind of confidence that came from knowing who she was. She was a lesbian, always had been. Roland respected that. He'd never so much as brushed her hand when they sat with tea between them.

But when he flicked the dial onto a new setting — one he'd cobbled together from a forum on "cellular resonance" — something shifted. The hum deepened, subtle but undeniable. His skin prickled. Her eyes darkened.

"Do you feel that?" she asked, shifting on the sofa.

He nodded. His cock was already hard, thickening against his trousers. He tried to hide it, but her gaze had dropped, and the silence between them pulsed heavier than the machine.

She licked her lips, almost dazed. "Roland... I don't..."

He reached for the dial to switch it off, but her hand caught his wrist. Strong. Shaking. She held him there.

Her thumb stroked over his skin once, twice, and then her eyes were on his mouth.

The kiss was sudden. Hot. Wrong. Her tongue pushed into his mouth with desperate hunger, her body pressing into his. He groaned, feeling her breasts crush against his chest.

His hands roamed without thought — under her top, finding the soft weight of her tits. Her nipples were already hard, pebbling against his palms. She moaned into his mouth as he squeezed them, harder than he should have, but she arched into it.

"Fuck... I can't stop..." she gasped, fumbling at his belt. Her hand slipped inside, wrapping around his cock, stroking it with frantic need.

He groaned, thrusting into her fist, the machine's low throb coursing through him. He slid his own hand under her jeans, under her knickers, and found her cunt soaking. Slick. Burning.

"Christ, Sam..."

Her answer was a guttural moan. She straddled him, yanking her jeans down just enough, grinding her wet slit against his cock. He pushed her knickers aside and shoved into her in one rough thrust.

Her scream filled the room. "Oh god—Roland—fuck!"

They moved like animals. No tenderness, no thought. Just raw, furious rutting. The sofa cushions slid to the floor as she rode him, tits bouncing, hair plastered to her face with sweat. He gripped her ass, driving her down harder onto his cock, each slap of flesh loud in the charged air.

Her nails raked his shoulders. Her cunt clenched, milking him. She came with a shuddering cry, grinding down on him as juices spilled hot around his cock. The sight, the sound, the impossible reality of it — it dragged him over with her.

He roared, thrusting deep, spilling inside her in thick, pulsing waves.

When it was over, she collapsed against him, both of them panting, the machine still humming softly in the background as if nothing had happened.

Sam's voice was hoarse when she whispered, "What the hell did you do to us?"

Roland looked at the dial glowing faintly in the dark. His cock was still half-hard inside her, throbbing.

He had one reply 'Three. Point-three'
But he knew this was only the beginning.

✦ ✦ ✦

Chapter One
The Machine

Two Weeks earlier

Roland never liked to think of himself as gullible. He'd lived sixty years without chasing fads or miracle cures. He balanced his accounts to the penny, changed light bulbs before they burned out, and never bought anything online without first reading every review twice. But pain could wear down even the most practical of men, and the ache in his shoulders had been constant for over a decade.

It wasn't crippling, not exactly. Just a stiff, grinding soreness that made mornings miserable and nights restless. Pills dulled it, but the relief was temporary. Physio had helped, until the NHS waiting list stretched so far he gave up trying. He hated to admit it, but he had begun to live around the ache, as if his world had grown smaller to fit his failing joints.

So when the advert appeared on his computer — tucked between gardening tools and arthritis supplements — Roland had paused.

Scalar resonance therapy. Tune the body back into balance. Natural relief, no side effects.

He'd scoffed at first, muttering "quackery" under his breath. Yet he clicked the link. The page was plain, almost austere, with none of the glossy salesmanship he expected. A box, two slender towers, and a handful of lines promising *results you can feel*.

Three days later, curiosity won.

The parcel arrived in a nondescript brown box. No logo, no branding, nothing to betray what sat inside. Roland slit the tape with a kitchen knife and peeled back the cardboard to reveal dense grey foam. Nestled within were three objects.

The first was the generator: a brushed metal box the size of a shoebox, heavier than it looked. Two chunky black dials jutted from the front, framing a small green digital display that blinked uncertainly when he pressed the switch. A low hum rose at once, steady and almost soothing.

The other two pieces were the towers — thin metal tubes, each about two feet tall, capped with small bulbs that glowed faintly once connected. They were surprisingly light, almost delicate, with coiled wires running down to a single jack that slotted neatly into the back of the generator.

At the bottom of the box sat a folded leaflet, more pamphlet than manual. Roland unfolded it, frowning at the sparse instructions.

Place towers opposite each other. Field strongest between. Tune frequency as required. The body will respond.

That was it. No diagrams, no health disclaimers, no warnings. Just a promise that the "body would know."

Roland chuckled. "Well, that's bloody helpful."

Still, he carried the towers into the living room and set them on either side of his old armchair, facing each other across the rug. He perched the generator on the coffee table, fiddled with the dials, and flicked the switch.

The bulbs glowed. The hum steadied. The air between the towers felt... charged, somehow. Nothing visible, yet when he walked between them the hairs on his forearms lifted as though brushed by static.

He lowered himself into the armchair, wincing at the familiar grind in his shoulders. The ache was there, as always. He sat for ten minutes, listening to the hum, adjusting the dials until the pitch deepened and softened again.

Then he realised: the ache had dulled. Not vanished, but eased, as if someone had turned the volume down by a single notch.

Roland leaned back, surprised. It could have been coincidence. Placebo. Wishful thinking. But it was enough to keep him sitting until the generator's timer clicked off.

Over the next week, the machine became part of his evenings. He brewed tea, turned on the news, then settled between the towers with his battered spiral-bound notebook.

He treated it like an experiment. Each page filled with neat columns of numbers, times, and comments:

Setting 7.4 – mild warmth in knees.
8.0 – no noticeable change.
9.2 – shoulders eased within five minutes.
10.1 – faint tingling in hands.

Most of the entries were dull, but now and then something strange appeared.

12.3 – odd buzzing in teeth.
12.7 – brief dizziness, posture straighter after.
13.2 – chest felt heavy, eased when switched off.

He told himself it was imagination, the product of sitting too long in silence. Still, the pages filled quickly, and he found himself oddly eager to try again each night.

Sam noticed first.

She was watering her hanging baskets one afternoon when she leaned over the garden fence. "What's that contraption you've been fiddling with, Roland?"

Sam had been his neighbour for nearly six years. Early thirties, sharp-tongued, always ready with a joke. Short dark hair that never stayed flat, and a smile that came easily, though it carried a glint of mischief.

Roland smiled back. "Just a health gadget. Scalar energy therapy, they call it."

"Scalar what now?"

"Two towers, a generator, a field between them. I sit in the middle, twiddle the dials, see what happens."

She raised an eyebrow. "Sounds like snake oil."

"Could be," he admitted. "But my shoulders don't ache as much when I use it."

She smirked. "If you start glowing in the dark, don't say I didn't warn you."

Roland chuckled, but her teasing stayed with him. Snake oil or not, the machine was doing something.

It was late one evening, rain lashing against the windows, when Roland decided to test the machine's limits.

The leaflet had said simply: *place towers opposite each other.* But how far apart could they be?

He carried one tower into the hallway, leaving the other in its usual spot. The generator buzzed, the bulbs glowed, and Roland stepped carefully into the middle of the invisible line.

The sensation came instantly: a tingling rush down his arms, stronger than he'd felt before. Surprised, he scribbled quickly in his notebook. *Field present even when towers separated. Strength increased. Investigate further.*

The next evening, he went further. One tower in the lounge, the other in the kitchen. He paced back and forth, through the archway, and still the tingling remained, faint at the edges but undeniable in the middle.

By the third night, he carried one tower upstairs, balancing it on the bedside cabinet. He stood halfway up the staircase, tea in hand, feeling the buzz ripple over him.

He laughed aloud, shaking his head. "Bloody nonsense," he muttered, though his pen was already moving: *Distance does not break field. Range greater than expected. Possible entire house affected.*

When Sam saw him dragging one tower across the drive the next day, she shook her head. "Honestly, Roland, you look like you're building a teleport machine."

Roland grinned. "You joke, but I think this thing's stronger than it looks. Doesn't matter how far apart the towers are — the field's still there."

She folded her arms, sceptical. "So your whole house is buzzing now?"

"Not just the house. I reckon it works anywhere between them. I could put one tower in my shed and the other in the spare room, and the field would cover the whole garden."

Sam laughed. "Well, if you vanish in a puff of smoke, at least I'll know where to look."

Roland smiled, but later, when the machine was humming again, her words echoed in his head.

That night, lying in bed long after the generator was off, Roland felt it still: a faint vibration under his skin, like the echo of a tuning fork.

It wasn't pain. It wasn't even unpleasant. Just a thrum, steady and insistent, as though the space between the towers had followed him upstairs and settled in his chest.

He turned onto his side, staring into the dark.

The leaflet had said *the body will respond.*

Roland wondered, not for the first time, whether the machine was doing more than soothing his shoulders.

Whether, perhaps, it was only just beginning.

Chapter Two
The First Signals

Roland set the notebook on his lap, tapping the pen against the page. The generator purred on the table beside him, the towers glowing faintly across the room. He had run enough trials now to know the field wasn't limited to a neat corridor between the towers.

Walls meant nothing.

He had proved it the night before, carrying one tower into the shed while the other remained in the lounge. When he walked through the kitchen — twenty feet from either device — the tingling still crawled over his arms, stronger than ever.

This evening, he had tested again. One tower in the lounge, the other upstairs in the spare room. He'd stood on the landing, nowhere near either, and still the invisible current had fizzed across his skin.

Roland rubbed his temples, staring at the green numbers on the generator. *Field covers entire bungalow. No shield. Cannot avoid once activated.*

The discovery unsettled him. He had thought of the machine as a tool, controllable, something he could switch on and off like a heater. But now he realised: once the towers were live, the whole house was saturated. There was no hiding from it.

It was during one of these late experiments that Roland stumbled across the frequency. He hadn't meant to find it. He had been drifting up and down the scale, logging sensations — warmth, tingling, dizziness — when the hum shifted into something deeper, almost physical in his chest.

Then it spread lower.

A glow unfurled in his belly, heavy and insistent. His cock stirred.

Roland froze, breath catching. Erections had been rare for years, unreliable at best. He had quietly accepted it as part of age — something gone, not coming back. But now, within seconds, he was hard.

Not half, not fleeting. Full. Thick. Pressing against the inside of his trousers with a force that made him groan aloud.

"Jesus Christ," he muttered, fumbling for the dial. He turned it down sharply. The hum eased, and so did he — softening, the heat ebbing away.

He stared at the generator, stunned.

Heart hammering, he turned the dial back up. The hum deepened. The warmth flared instantly, and his cock surged back to full strength, straining almost painfully against the zip.

He sat there gasping, eyes wide, as if his own body were betraying him.

"Bloody hell," he whispered.

His pen scratched hurriedly across the page: *Frequency 14.6 – sexual arousal. Immediate erection. Strong, sustained. No comparable experience in years.*

Roland snapped the switch off and pushed back from the chair, trembling. He had never felt so alive — and so unsettled.

He tried to ignore it for days, keeping the generator at safer settings. But the knowledge gnawed at him, a temptation impossible to forget.

When Sam leaned over the fence a few evenings later, her sharp eyes on the living room window, Roland felt the confession rising before he could stop it.

"You've been at that thing every night," she teased. "What's it really doing to you?"

He cleared his throat. "You'll laugh."

"Try me."

Roland lowered his voice, glancing around though no one else was near. "It's not just pain relief. I've... found another setting. One that does something else."

"Such as?"

His face burned. "It... stirs things. Things I thought were gone for good."

Sam's eyebrow arched. "You mean it got your cock working again?"

Roland winced at her bluntness but nodded. "Yes. Stronger than I've felt in years."

She stared at him for a moment, half amused, half sceptical. Then she laughed, shaking her head. "So your magic towers double as Viagra now? Christ, Roland."

"I'm not joking, Sam. It's real."

She had laughed at first — of course she had — but her curiosity got the better of her. "Fine," she'd said at the fence, folding her arms. "Leave me in your lounge with your magic towers. You step out. I'll sit. And afterwards I'll tell you the truth."

That evening, Roland set the towers in their usual places and showed her how the generator worked. "Once I start it, I'll go outside. The field fills the whole house. I can't be in here without…" He cleared his throat. "Without reacting."

Her lips quirked. "Understood. Go wait in the garden. I'll knock when I'm done."

She sat back in his armchair, jeans hugging her thighs, dark hair falling loose around her face. She crossed her arms, sceptical.

Roland hesitated, hand on the dial. "Ready?"

"Ready."

He turned it slowly to 14.6. The hum deepened. The bulbs on the towers glowed soft gold. At once he felt the pulse stir in his own body, and he quickly slipped out the door, pulling it shut behind him.

Inside, Sam exhaled sharply.

At first it was nothing more than a faint buzz in her skin, like the mild static before a storm. She had half a mind to laugh, to call Roland back in and tell him he'd wasted his money.

But then the sensation spread.

A warmth coiled low in her belly, subtle at first, then sharper, as if invisible fingers traced down her spine and across her thighs. Her nipples stiffened against her shirt, sudden and aching.

Her eyes fluttered shut. The hum wasn't just in the air — it was inside her. Each breath carried the vibration deeper, winding into places she hadn't expected.

Her thighs pressed together without thought. The heat grew heavier, pulsing, insistently alive.

Sam bit her lip. She had told Roland she'd prove him wrong, that she'd feel nothing. But her body was betraying her, betraying years of certainty, betraying even the identity she had carried proudly.

She shifted in the chair, jeans suddenly too tight. A faint dampness spread between her legs. She let out a soft sound, startled, and clamped her mouth shut.

The hum only deepened. Her nipples throbbed now, her cunt slick, and she felt the ache to move — to rub, to grind, to do something to answer the field's demand.

Her breath quickened, chest rising and falling. "Bloody hell," she whispered, the words catching in her throat.

She forced her eyes open, dragging herself upright. Her hands trembled as she pushed her hair back. "Enough," she muttered. "Enough."

She opened the front door sharply, cool night air rushing against her flushed skin. Roland stood waiting, notebook in hand, face tense.

"Well?" he asked.

Sam swallowed, cheeks hot. "I felt it."

"Where?" His voice cracked slightly.

She hesitated. Her pride wanted to dismiss it, to call it static and nothing more. But honesty slipped out before she could stop it. "Everywhere. Heat. Tingling. My—" She stopped herself, shaking her head. "Lower too. Strong."

Roland nodded slowly, pen scratching. "So it isn't just me."

She folded her arms, defensive. "Don't read into it. It was… odd. That's all."

But the way her thighs pressed together, the way her breath still came quick — those betrayed more than her words ever could.

When Roland shut down the generator and returned to his notes later, his hand shook.

Sam confirms arousal. Heat, nipples sensitive, moisture reported indirectly. Effects undeniable.

He stared at the words until they blurred.

The machine wasn't only a curiosity now. It was doing something deeper, something neither of them could ignore.

Chapter Three
Thirty-Three Point Three

Roland had begun to trust his notebook more than the leaflet. The pamphlet had been vague to the point of uselessness, but his scrawled observations built a picture, line by line, of what the machine could do.

Heat. Tingling. Pressure. Arousal.

Yet nothing prepared him for the night he found 3.3.

He had been drifting slowly up and down the scale, dials steady beneath his fingers, when the hum changed. It was not louder, not sharper, but different — a resonance that seemed to settle into his bones and vibrate outward.

The sensation was immediate, stronger than anything he had logged before. His skin prickled. His chest fluttered as though a hand pressed against his sternum. And lower — God, lower — his cock surged to life so violently he gasped.

It wasn't the sharp rush of 14.6. This was heavier, deeper, like his entire body was being tuned to one undeniable note.

He lasted less than a minute before snapping the switch off, trembling.

The numbers glowed faintly on the display: **3.3**.

Roland stared at them, pulse hammering. He didn't write it in the notebook. Not yet. Some instinct told him to keep it to himself.

The next day, Sam appeared at the fence again, as if she had been waiting for him.

"So, Professor," she teased, "found any new tricks with your towers?"

Roland swallowed. "Maybe. A frequency I haven't shown you yet."

Her eyebrow lifted. "Oh? And what does this one do?"

"I can't quite explain it." He looked away. "But it's stronger. More... insistent."

Sam smirked, but her eyes glinted with curiosity. "Then let's test it."

That evening she settled into his armchair once more.

"Same rules," Roland said firmly. "I'll switch it on, then go outside. The field covers the whole place. I can't stay in here."

"Fine by me." She tugged her shirt straight, crossing her legs. "Set your magic number and let's see."

Roland's hand hovered on the dial. He turned it. "Three point three."

The hum deepened, different from before — slower, heavier, almost like a heartbeat pulsing through the air.

The towers glowed, the bungalow thick with invisible current.

Roland felt the first stirrings in his own body and quickly slipped out the door, closing it behind him.

Inside, Sam stiffened in the chair.

The first wave was a rush of heat, flooding her belly and thighs. It wasn't gentle this time — it was immediate, surging, like a switch had been flipped inside her. Her nipples tightened painfully beneath her shirt. Her cunt throbbed, wetness blooming at once between her legs.

She gasped, clutching the arms of the chair.

"Fucking hell…" she whispered.

She tried to resist, tried to focus on the hum, the glow, anything but the ache between her legs. But it was no use. Her thighs pressed together, squirming. Her clit pulsed, demanding friction.

She moaned, shocked by the sound. "Oh God—"

Her hand moved before she could stop it, sliding between her jeans, pressing against the swollen heat. The field pulsed harder, insistent, relentless.

Her fingers rubbed, frantic, hips lifting off the chair. Her breath tore in quick gasps, body trembling.

She came hard, sudden, with a cry she barely muffled against her wrist. The orgasm ripped through her, clenching, soaking her knickers as she writhed against her own hand.

The hum filled her ears. Her pulse thundered. Her body sagged boneless into the chair, sweat damp on her temples.

When she could finally move, she lurched to her feet, tugged her clothes straight, and stumbled to the door.

Roland stood waiting in the dark, notebook clutched in one hand. Sam emerged flushed, hair sticking damply to her forehead, eyes wide with something between shock and awe.

He opened his mouth, but she cut him off with a hoarse laugh.

"Roland... what the hell was that?"

He cleared his throat. "Three point Three."

She stared at him, chest still rising and falling. "You need to show me how it works. Every setting. Every dial."

Roland hesitated.

Her lips curved into a fierce smile. "And when you're not using it... can I borrow it?"

Roland nodded slowly, though his chest felt tight.

Because he knew then: this wasn't just his machine anymore.

Chapter Four
The Proposal

Roland thought Sam might laugh the whole thing off after what happened at 3.3. But the very next afternoon she leaned over the fence, eyes bright.

"I've had an idea," she said. "I'm hosting a little get-together next weekend. Drinks, music, a few friends. Why don't you bring the machine over?"

Roland choked on his tea. "Bring it over? What for?"

"So they can feel it," Sam said, grinning. "You saw what it did to me. Imagine a whole lounge full of people inside that field. It'll be unforgettable."

His chest tightened. "Sam, this isn't a toy. It's not... safe."

"Safe?" She gave a short laugh. "Come on, Roland. Nobody fainted. Nobody exploded. I just—" She stopped herself, colour rising to her cheeks. "I just felt something stronger than I've ever felt before. That's exactly why I want it."

Roland shook his head. "I don't know."

"Then show me," she pressed. "Teach me how to work it properly this week. If I know what I'm doing, you won't have to worry."

That evening, Roland carried the generator and towers the short walk across her lawn. Sam cleared her dining table, watching eagerly as he set the pieces down.

"First rule," Roland said, placing the towers opposite each other, "they must always face each other. Doesn't matter how far apart — the field fills the whole space between. Through walls, through doors. Once they're live, your entire house will be in it."

Sam nodded, lips pursed in concentration.

"This dial," Roland went on, tapping the generator, "controls frequency. Lower bands relax you. Fourteen-point-six... arousal. Three-point-three—" He stopped.

Her grin widened. "That's the one that made me lose control."

Roland ignored the remark, pointing at the second dial. "This is intensity. Keep it low. Too high and you'll overwhelm people. You don't want your party ending in panic."

She smirked. "Depends what kind of panic."

He glared. "I'm serious, Sam."

"I know," she said softly, though her smile never faded.

They practised over the next few nights. Roland showed her how to set the dials, how to reset the generator if it stalled. Sam scribbled mock-scientific notes in a pad of her own, deliberately exaggerating:

7.5 — tingles. 14.6 — erections. 3.3 — mind blown.

Roland scowled at her handwriting. "You're not taking this seriously."

"Oh, I am," she said with a mischievous gleam. "Just in my own way."

One evening she flicked too high on the dial, and the air between them pulsed at once. Sam gasped, bracing herself on the table, while Roland felt the unmistakable surge of heat rising through his body.

He lunged to switch it off. "Careful!"

She laughed shakily, cheeks flushed. "Bloody hell. You weren't exaggerating."

"That's exactly why you need to control it."

"I will," she promised. Then, eyes glinting: "Next weekend, this house is going to be very interesting."

When Roland left, crossing back over the fence to his own kitchen, his stomach was tight with dread.

Because part of him wanted to keep the machine locked away forever.

And another part — darker, hungrier — wanted to see what would happen when a whole roomful of bodies were caught in the field of three point three.

✦ ✦ ✦

Chapter Five

The Eve

Friday evening found Roland in Sam's lounge, kneeling by the generator for what he told himself would be the last time. The towers stood on either side of the room, angled just right, their tips faintly glinting in the lamplight.

"Straight line, level," he muttered, adjusting the left one a fraction. He tapped the cable, checked the socket, then jotted a note. "All fine."

Sam lounged on the sofa, sipping a glass of wine, watching him with amusement.

"You know, Roland, you fuss over this thing like it's a newborn."

He scowled, tightening the dial. "Because it's not a toy. One wrong setting and—"

"And everyone gets a bit tingly?" she cut in, grinning. "Relax. It'll be fun."

Roland stood, dusting off his knees. "Fun isn't the word I'd use."

She raised her glass, eyes glinting. "Tomorrow night, you'll thank me."

They ran a short test — low frequency, low intensity. The towers hummed softly, the air thickened, and the faint vibration crept across Roland's skin. He snapped it off before it went further.

"Everything works," he said curtly.

"Good," Sam replied, stretching like a cat. "Because tomorrow there'll be ten of us in here. Music, drink, laughter… and that." She nodded at the generator. "Imagine it, Roland. A roomful of people who don't even know what's coming, or who.' She giggled.

He swallowed. "That's what worries me."

She smirked. "That's what excites me."

Later, back in his own bungalow, Roland sat at the kitchen table, staring at his notebook. The line he hadn't dared write still burned in his mind: *3.3 — irresistible compulsion. Total surrender.*

He closed the book and leaned back, eyes closing.

And the fantasies came.

He imagined Sam's lounge full of bodies, chatter fading as the hum deepened. A woman laughing mid-sentence, then faltering, her eyes widening as her nipples hardened beneath her blouse. A man clutching his drink too tightly as his cock stiffened in his trousers. Pairs shifting closer on the sofa, thighs pressing together, breath quickening in the thick, invisible heat.

He pictured hands fumbling at zips, dresses tugged upward, kisses stolen in the charged air. Sam herself, flushed and grinning, watching her friends come undone in her lounge.

Roland's cock stirred, heavy and urgent. He shifted in his chair, ashamed and aroused in equal measure.

Tomorrow night it would no longer be fantasy.

The house next door would be alive with the hum of 3.3.

And Roland would be close enough to hear every sound.

✦ ✦ ✦

Chapter Six
The Party

Saturday evening settled cool and quiet over the gardens. From his kitchen, Roland heard the faint pulse of music from Sam's lounge, bursts of laughter, the clink of bottles. For hours it was nothing unusual — friends chatting, glasses refilling.

But close to midnight, the sound shifted.

The music dipped, voices hushed, and Roland felt it — a pressure in his chest, a tremor in his blood. Sam had switched the generator on.

He stood, restless, and that was when he saw it: her lounge curtain left half open, exactly where his own kitchen window faced. From here, with his light off, he had a clear view inside. As if she had meant him to.

At first it was subtle — guests fidgeting, tugging at collars, thighs pressing together. A woman let out a shaky laugh, another leaned closer to the man beside her.

Then the field took hold.

Bodies entwined, kisses stolen. Shirts ripped open. Bras tugged aside. The sofa became a tangle of mouths and hands, the armchair a frantic coupling.

Roland's cock stiffened at once, throbbing against his trousers. He pressed closer to the glass, heart hammering.

And then Sam.

She was no longer standing with wine in hand. The field had her, too. Her cheeks were flushed, eyes wild, her body moving with an urgency Roland had never seen in her.

A man gripped her waist, trousers half-down, cock jutting hard. Sam straddled him without hesitation, tugging her jeans aside and sinking down in one fierce thrust.

Roland's jaw slackened.

She cried out, riding him hard, tits bouncing free under her shirt. Her head tipped back, sweat gleaming at her throat, hair sticking to her temples. She ground down on him with desperate hunger, her cunt swallowing his cock over and over.

Lesbian or not, in the field it meant nothing. The machine stripped everything away but raw need.

Roland unzipped himself with trembling fingers, cock thick and urgent in his hand. He pumped hard, eyes fixed on her as the room erupted around her — men groaning, women moaning, bodies colliding in every corner.

On the rug, a woman was bent forward, taking cock from behind while another licked between her legs. On the sofa, two men jerked each other off while watching Sam ride, their faces flushed, cocks glistening.

But Roland saw only her. Sam bouncing on that man's lap, her breasts jiggling with every slam down, her mouth open in an unashamed scream.

And then, as if sensing him, she turned.

Her gaze slid to the open curtain, straight across the dark garden to his kitchen window. Roland froze, hand still stroking his cock. He couldn't tell if she could see him — the light was off, the glass reflecting — but her eyes lingered, locked in his direction.

Roland moaned, pumping faster, his forehead pressed to the cold pane.

Inside, Sam's nails raked the man's chest, her cunt clenching visibly around his cock as she ground harder, staring towards the window all the while.

It was deliberate. She knew.

And Roland, cock in fist, watching his lesbian neighbour ride a man to pieces while staring right at him, felt release boiling, unstoppable.

He came with a stifled roar, spilling hot cum over his hand, never looking away from her.

The lounge remained a frenzy, the field pulsing stronger with every thrust, every scream.

And Roland sagged against the window, chest heaving, as Sam threw her head back and came hard on another man's cock — knowing he was watching.

Roland's climax left him trembling, forehead pressed against the cold kitchen glass, hand sticky with cum. But the sounds spilling across the garden didn't stop — they swelled, thick and relentless.

Moans, cries, the slap of flesh on flesh.

His cock, still damp in his grip, twitched again. He groaned softly, ashamed and aroused in equal measure. It wasn't enough. Not nearly enough.

He needed to see more.

He slipped out his back door, easing it shut without a sound. The night air was cool, sharp in his lungs, but the hum of the generator pulsed through him all the same. The field reached him even here, thickening his blood, stirring heat back into his groin.

He crept closer, keeping to the shadows, until Sam's open curtain filled his view.

And there it was.

The lounge was chaos. Naked bodies sprawled across the furniture, limbs tangled, skin glistening. The air inside seemed almost smoky with heat, the rhythm of the field pressing everyone into a fever.

On the rug, a woman lay on her back, legs spread wide, while another knelt between them, working a pink vibrator against her swollen clit. The woman writhed, tits bouncing as she screamed, her juices slick across her thighs.

Nearby, two men fucked one woman at once — one taking her from behind, cock pounding her cunt, while the other thrust into her mouth, holding her head in place as she gagged around him. Her eyes rolled back, body trembling under their grip.

Roland's cock hardened again, impossibly quick, pressing against the damp fabric of his trousers.

And then Sam again.

She was on her knees now, bent over the arm of the sofa, a man behind her driving into her cunt with brutal thrusts. Her moans tore the air, sharp and raw, her tits swinging beneath her with each slam forward.

Another woman leaned over her, pressing a buzzing toy against Sam's clit as she was fucked. Sam's body jolted, nails clawing at the cushions.

Roland's breath caught. His neighbour — thirty-two, beautiful, always confident and untouchable — was now a wild, sweat-soaked vision, being fucked hard while toys buzzed against her.

And still, as her body convulsed in another climax, her head turned toward the window.

Straight toward him.

Roland stumbled closer to the hedge, breath ragged, cock gripped tight in his hand as he pumped furiously, eyes locked on the younger woman writhing under cock and toy alike.

He didn't know if she could truly see him in the darkness — but God help him, he hoped she could.

Roland edged closer, the hedge brushing against his arm as he moved right up to the lounge window. He stayed low, crouched in the shadows, breath hot and ragged in the cool night air.

The hum of the machine throbbed through him, his cock stiff and slick in his fist, each pump pulling another gasp from his chest.

Inside, the orgy raged. Bodies twisted together, sweat gleaming, toys buzzing. Flesh slapped, moans tangled, the room a writhing knot of raw desire.

And then Sam.

She had slipped free from the man who'd been pounding her, collapsing back onto the sofa with her legs spread wide. Her face was flushed, hair wild, tits still bouncing from the aftershocks of orgasm.

Slowly, almost lazily, she brought her hand between her thighs.

Roland's breath caught as she dipped two fingers into her soaked cunt, curling them deep, then slid them back out glistening.

And with a sly smile, she lifted them to her lips.

She sucked them clean, eyes fluttering shut at first —
then opening again, her gaze sliding across the room,
out the half-open curtain.

Straight to where Roland crouched in the darkness.

He froze, cock tight in his hand, unsure if she could see
him. The shadows cloaked him, the kitchen lights were
off — but Sam's eyes lingered, and her tongue swept
slowly over her fingers, lapping her own taste with
deliberate hunger.

Roland groaned silently, pumping harder, every nerve
on fire. His neighbour — thirty-two, always
untouchable, always just beyond him — was now
spread and slick, licking herself clean while looking
right where he hid.

It wasn't an accident.

She knew.

And Roland, trembling in the shadows, spilled his cum
across the grass, never breaking her gaze.

✦ ✦ ✦

Chapter Seven
The Knock

Roland spent most of the morning in a fog. He tried to busy himself — the crossword, washing the dishes, even trimming the hedge — but his mind refused to settle. Every idle moment replayed the same scenes: Sam astride a man, tits bouncing, eyes wild. Sam licking her own fingers, gaze sliding to the half-open curtain. Sam's smile as if she knew.

He had come twice more that morning, shame hot in his veins, standing over the sink with his trousers around his knees, unable to stop remembering. At sixty years old, he thought those days were long behind him. Yet the machine had rewired him, set him aflame.

By early afternoon he was brewing another cup of tea, telling himself the worst of it was over. That's when he heard it: a firm knock at his kitchen window.

Roland spun, nearly spilling the pot.

Sam stood there, leaning on the sill as if she had all the time in the world. Her hair was tied up today, loose strands framing her face. She wore faded jeans and a white vest top, no bra — her nipples faintly pressing against the fabric in the daylight. Casual, effortless, younger than ever.

Roland swallowed hard, sliding the window open. "Afternoon, Sam."

"Afternoon, neighbour." Her tone was breezy, teasing. "Hope I'm not disturbing you."

"Not at all," he said quickly.

"I thought I should bring this back." She bent out of sight, then straightened again with the generator in her hands. The leads and towers rested on the grass behind her. "Wouldn't want to keep your baby too long."

Roland's heart gave a thump as he reached out to steady it. "Yes, of course. Thank you."

"Don't thank me," she said, lips quirking. "I should be the one thanking you. It was…" Her eyes lingered on his. "…a fantastic night."

Roland set the generator on the counter, clearing his throat. "I'm glad it… went smoothly."

"Smoothly?" She laughed under her breath. "That's not the word I'd use. Nothing about it was smooth. It was raw. Messy. Completely unforgettable."

He shifted in his seat, heat creeping up his neck.

Sam leaned on the sill again, resting her chin in her palm. "You know, I've hosted plenty of little get-togethers here before. Same routine. People drinking, gossiping, glancing at the time. But last night…" She shook her head, smile widening. "Last night they didn't want to leave. People were begging for one more drink, one more song. One more… something."

Roland swallowed. "Yes, well… that's what happens when resonance builds."

"Resonance." She repeated it slowly, rolling the word on her tongue. "I like that. Resonance." Her eyes glittered, and the pause that followed was heavy, deliberate.

Roland's throat felt dry. He sipped his tea, trying not to stare at her chest through the vest.

Sam went on, voice low and conversational. "Funny thing is, I don't remember much after midnight. Not clearly. Just flashes. Bodies. Heat. Sounds. Like it all melted together. It's strange, isn't it? When you know you've done something outrageous… but you can't bring yourself to feel guilty for it."

Roland nodded mutely.

Her gaze flicked to him again. "Of course, you probably already know that."

His heart stumbled. "What do you mean?"

"Oh, nothing." She waved a hand airily, but the smirk remained. "Just saying. You've got that look. Like a man who already knows more than he lets on."

Roland forced a laugh, awkward, transparent.

Sam didn't press. She just let the silence hum between them, her eyes resting on him with calm certainty, as if she could hear every thought in his head.

Chapter Eight
The Proposal

Roland had barely sat down in his armchair when there came another knock — this time at the door. He opened it to find Sam leaning casually against the frame, as though she owned the place. Loose blouse, denim shorts, hair tied up again, and that same playful sparkle in her eyes.

"Mind if I come in?" she asked, already stepping past him.

Roland closed the door with a sigh. "What is it this time?"

She perched on the edge of his kitchen table, legs swinging, gaze flicking to the generator resting on his counter. "Last night was… incredible."

Roland bristled. "It got out of hand."

Her smile curved. "That's the point. And now the genie's out of the bottle, Roland. One of my friends — you probably noticed her, red hair, black dress — she's already asked about hiring it. She knows people who'd kill for an experience like that."

His stomach tightened. "Hire it out? Absolutely not."

"Not to just anyone," Sam soothed. "Think bigger. Think… selective. Exclusive. People with money, taste, connections. Imagine what it could mean for you."

She slid closer, lowering her voice. "I'm not talking about more Saturday-night house parties. I'm talking about villas in Spain, seaside mansions, old country manors where the rich and bored gather behind locked gates. Can you picture it? Silk curtains, marble floors, guests in gowns and tuxedos… until you turn the dial."

Roland blinked, throat dry.

Sam leaned back against the counter, arms folded under her breasts. "Or castles. Real ones. Firelight, vaulted ceilings, echoes of moans bouncing off stone walls while people who've never said no in their lives finally lose every scrap of control. They'd pay a fortune for that. And you — the man behind the curtain, the one who makes it possible — you'd be there, watching it unfold."

Roland tried to laugh, but it came out weak. "You're fantasising."

"Am I?" Her gaze pinned him. "Because last night was just a bungalow with a few friends, and even that nearly broke you. Imagine what it would do when the playground is bigger. When the people are hungrier."

Roland gripped the arms of his chair. The images flooded him in spite of himself: chandeliers glittering above writhing bodies, garden parties dissolving into shameless tangles on manicured lawns, stately bedrooms echoing with screams of pleasure. Sam's voice wove around his thoughts, feeding the fantasy.

"You think you've seen it all?" she whispered. "You haven't. You've only opened the door. There are people out there — beautiful, powerful, untouchable — who spend their lives chasing something that can't be bought. But this…" She tapped the generator. "This is the key. You hold it. And if you let them step inside your field, Roland, they'll pay you whatever you ask. In money. In favours. In… experiences."

Her lips quirked, eyes sliding over him with wicked intent. "All your wildest dreams. Every secret desire. Fulfilled."

Roland's cock stirred traitorously in his trousers. He shifted, praying she hadn't noticed.

She leaned down, close to his ear, her voice a purr. "Last night was proof. You saw what happened. You 'watched.' You didn't think I left the curtain open by mistake, did you?"

Roland's breath caught.

Sam's smile deepened. "Exactly. I wanted you to see. And now I want you to imagine more. Bigger. Richer. Wilder. A thousand nights like that, in places you've only ever dreamed of."

She straightened, brushing invisible dust from her shorts. "All you have to do, Roland, is say yes."

When she left, the house fell silent again — but Roland was no longer the same. His mind burned with visions of villas, castles, mansions, and the promise of endless, engineered abandon.

The machine sat on the counter, quiet, innocent.

But in Roland's imagination, it was already humming across the world.

And deep down, he already knew he'd give Sam her answer.

✦ ✦ ✦

Chapter Nine
The Argument

Roland sat stiffly in his chair, notebook open, pen idle. He had been trying to sketch out settings, frequencies, data — anything to remind himself the machine was just science, just a tool. Something to soothe aching joints, nothing more.

But the images wouldn't stop coming. The orgy. Sam's tits bouncing. Her eyes locking on him through the curtain.

He snapped the book shut.

"This has gone too far," he muttered aloud.

As if summoned, the knock came. Sam strolled in without waiting, blouse loose, shorts hugging her hips. She looked relaxed, but her eyes had that glint — the glint that always meant trouble.

"Afternoon, Roland." She glanced at the notebook. "Still scribbling numbers?"

He closed it quickly. "Sam, we need to stop this. It was never meant for that."

"For what?" she asked, leaning against the counter.

"For... what happened the other night. It was supposed to be about pain relief. My joints. My shoulders. That's all. Not…" His voice dropped. "Not that circus."

Her smile widened, slow and knowing. "Funny, I don't remember pain relief. I remember cocks. More cocks than I've ever seen in one place. I remember sucking them like I was starving. I remember being fucked until I couldn't breathe. And Roland…" She tilted her head. "I'm a lesbian."

He swallowed hard.

"Thirty-two years old," she went on softly, "and I've never so much as looked at a cock. But that field… God, it stripped me. It made me want it. Made me love it. And you know what? I didn't feel ashamed. I felt free."

Roland's hands trembled in his lap.

She stepped closer, voice lowering, each word deliberate.

"Imagine, Roland. If it did that to me… me, the girl who swore she'd never touch a man… what could it do to anyone? What could it do to you?"

He shook his head. "No. I can't. I won't. It's too dangerous."

But she didn't stop. She leaned on the table, eyes never leaving his, voice a whisper that cut straight through him.

"Imagine if it was just us. No party. No strangers. Just you and me, sitting in that field together. You, sixty, thinking your cock was finished. Me, young, lesbian, untouchable. And then the hum starts."

Roland's breath hitched.

Sam smiled wickedly. "Tell me you don't want to know what would happen."

The silence stretched between them, thick as the field itself.

Roland's cock stirred helplessly, betraying him.

And Sam saw it. Of course she did. Her grin widened, satisfied.

"You can resist all you like, Roland," she murmured, brushing past him toward the door. "But the machine doesn't lie. And neither does your body."

She left him there, shaking, hard, staring at the generator on the counter like it was the devil itself.

And in his mind, no matter how he fought it, the image burned bright: him and Sam, locked together in the hum of the field, unable to stop.

Roland had told himself it was finished. The machine was back on his counter, silent. The garden was dark. Sam had made her point and he would resist.

But sometime past midnight, when he wandered into the kitchen for water, his heart lurched.

The curtain.

Her lounge window was once again half open, spilling a warm slice of lamplight into the garden.

And inside, Roland froze.

Sam was kneeling on the sofa, head buried between her partner's thighs. The younger woman — blonde, slim, gasping — had her vest rucked up, tits bare, nipples stiff as Sam's mouth devoured her cunt.

The sounds carried faintly through the summer air: wet lapping, sharp little cries, the rustle of cushions.

Roland gripped the sill, cock stiffening instantly.

It was different from the party. There was no field, no hum, no machine. This was Sam as she really was — unapologetic, lesbian, ravenous for the taste of a woman.

Her tongue moved in slick, hungry circles, her jaw shining with wetness. The blonde writhed, moaning loudly, fingers twisted tight in Sam's dark hair. Sam's own breasts strained against her top, nipples hard as she ground herself against the cushions while licking harder.

Roland groaned under his breath, unzipping himself, stroking slow, his eyes locked on the scene.

The blonde cried out, thighs trembling, grinding her pussy hard against Sam's face. Sam didn't stop, sucking her clit noisily, then pulling back just long enough to lick her fingers and slide two deep into her lover's cunt.

The woman's scream filled the room, her back arching as she came, juices running over Sam's hand. Sam smiled, slick and glistening, then climbed up her body to kiss her deeply, tongues tangling, breasts pressed together.

Roland pumped his cock harder, chest heaving, the sight obscene and beautiful all at once.

And though Sam never once turned to the window, the open curtain, the angle of the light, the way her body was framed — it was too perfect to be chance.

She was pushing him. Testing him. Daring him.

And Roland knew, trembling as his cum spilled in the darkness, that it was only a matter of time before she'd take him further.

✦ ✦ ✦

Chapter Ten
The Confession

Roland was in the garden trimming his roses when he heard her voice.

"Morning, neighbour."

He turned, secateurs in hand. Sam leaned on the fence, arms folded, hair loose around her cheeks. She wore leggings and a cropped hoodie, casual, fresh-faced — and yet her smirk made his stomach knot instantly.

"Morning," he muttered, snipping a stem too short.

Sam's eyes glinted. "Sleep well?"

"As well as I could," Roland said stiffly.

"Mm." She tilted her head. "Funny thing. My curtain was open again last night."

Roland froze.

Sam's grin widened. "I wonder who might have been looking."

He coughed. "I—"

"Don't worry," she cut in smoothly. "I wanted you to. That's why I left it open. Twice now." Her voice softened, teasing. "And I have to say, Roland... knowing you were out there, watching while I had my face buried between her thighs... well, it made it even hotter."

Roland's cock twitched traitorously. He shifted, flustered. "Sam, this has to stop."

She ignored him, stepping closer, resting her chin on the top of the fence. "You don't get it, do you? That machine of yours isn't just wires and dials. It's power. Real power. You've seen what it does — I've felt what it does. And now people are asking for it. Begging for it."

Roland shook his head. "It was never meant for that. It was for my joints. My shoulders. That's all."

Sam laughed, low and husky. "Your shoulders? Please. That thing made me suck cock like I'd been starving for it. I'm a lesbian, Roland. A lesbian. Do you know what it means that I was riding a man's cock, tits bouncing, screaming until my throat was raw? And loving every second of it?"

Roland swallowed hard, his hands trembling on the secateurs.

"Imagine," she pressed, voice dropping lower, "what happens when it's not just ten people in a lounge, but twenty in a villa. Or fifty in a manor. Imagine watching a castle full of bodies writhing, dripping, moaning — all because of you."

He shook his head firmly. "No. I don't want to be part of it."

Sam smirked. "But you already are."

Roland turned away, gripping the fence, but Sam's words slid into him like hooks. She leaned in, her voice soft, taunting.

"You can say no all you like. But I know you, Roland. I saw you. In the dark. Hand on your cock while I was spread across that sofa, licking her until she screamed."

His face burned, cock stiffening in betrayal.

Sam chuckled. "Yeah. You can deny the parties. Pretend you're too good for it. But you can't deny what it does to you. And sooner or later, you'll give in."

She pulled back, stretching lazily. "Anyway. Think about it. My friend's already waiting for an answer."

With that, she strolled back toward her house, hips swaying, leaving Roland trembling among his roses.

He stared down at his hands, the secateurs shaking.

She was right. He had been watching. He had been wanking.

And now, he wasn't sure if he could ever stop.

Roland stayed in the garden long after Sam disappeared, the weight of her words pressing down on him. He tried to busy himself, clipping deadheads, tidying the soil — but his hands trembled too much.

Finally, he went back inside, carried the generator and the towers into the loft, covering them with an old sheet. Out of sight, out of temptation. He stood there in the dust, breathing hard.

'Enough. No more. It wasn't meant for this.'

The thought of selling it crossed his mind. He could list it online, pass it off as a "frequency therapy unit," let it disappear into someone else's life. Someone else's problem. He'd walk away, wash his hands of the whole sordid business.

But when he climbed back down and shut the loft hatch, the silence in his bungalow was unbearable.

That night, lying in bed, the fantasies came back. Not about castles, villas, or Sam's friends. No — this was darker. More selfish.

What if he used it for himself?

Just himself.

No one needed to know. No parties, no gatherings. Just Roland in his bungalow, alone in the hum of 3.3. He could sit in the field, strip himself bare, and let it tear every inhibition out of him.

His cock stirred at the thought. He imagined the field making him ache, making him leak, forcing him to spill over and over until he couldn't take anymore. He imagined it wrapping around him like a lover, faceless but irresistible, turning him into a slave to his own need.

Roland groaned, rolling onto his side. Shame burned through him, but the dark thought clung stubbornly.

Maybe Sam was wrong. Maybe he didn't need her, or her friends, or her teasing little games.

Maybe the machine was never meant to be shared at all.

Maybe it was his. Only his.

✦ ✦ ✦

Chapter Eleven
The Lie

Roland waited until the evening, laptop shut, generator tucked away under its sheet. When the knock finally came, he already knew it would be Sam.

She leaned against the doorframe, casual as ever, eyes darting past him as if she expected to see the towers humming in his lounge.

"Well?" she asked. "Have you thought about it? My friend's waiting on an answer."

Roland forced a sigh. "You can tell her not to bother."

Sam frowned. "What do you mean?"

"I've sold it," he said evenly. "Online. Overseas buyer. Pick-up arranged. It's out of my hands now."

For the first time since he'd known her, Sam's confidence wavered. "You... you sold it?"

Roland nodded. "It was never meant for what you wanted. And frankly, I don't want to be mixed up in it anymore. I'll go back to my roses. You stick to your parties."

Sam studied him for a long moment, lips pressed tight. Then she gave a sharp little laugh, shaking her head. "You're mad. Absolutely mad. You had the world at your feet and you just gave it away."

"Better mad than ruined," Roland muttered.

She leaned closer, eyes narrowing. "You're lying. I can see it in your face. You didn't sell it."

"I did," Roland said firmly, meeting her gaze. "It's going."

The silence stretched. Finally, Sam huffed, turned on her heel, and stalked back down the path without another word.

Roland closed the door slowly, leaning his back against it. His heart hammered in his chest.

Because she was right. He hadn't sold it.

The generator was still in the loft. The towers were still his.

And now, without Sam's questions, her teasing, her friends, her parties — it was his secret alone.

Roland smiled faintly, a shadow crossing his face.

Now he could plan. Now he could choose.

And he already knew exactly the kind of women he wanted.

Young. Firm. Beautiful.

The kind who would never look twice at a man like him.

Until the field stripped them bare.

Roland stayed by the door long after Sam had gone, her words echoing in his head. 'You're lying. I can see it in your face.'

He shook himself. He had been convincing enough. She'd think him a fool, not a liar. That was good. That gave him time.

But not safety.

If he kept the machine here, sooner or later Sam would spot something. A hum through the wall. A glow through the curtains. She might even try to catch him out.

No, the bungalow was no longer safe.

If he was to pursue this — properly pursue it — he would need somewhere else.

He sat at his kitchen table, pouring himself a whisky, notebook open. At the top of the page, in careful block letters, he wrote:

LOCATIONS.

And beneath it:

- *Too close = risk (Sam).*
- *Need privacy.*
- *Easy access.*
- *Discreet.*

He thought of places he knew. The old lock-up garages on the edge of town — too damp, too exposed. The church hall — no chance, too public. His allotment shed — laughable, no power supply.

Then his mind turned darker.

There were plenty of empty spaces in this town. Unused rooms above shops. A cottage half-abandoned near the river. Even the big Victorian villa on Hatherley Road that had been empty since its owner died last winter.

Yes. Somewhere like that. Dusty. Forgotten. Private.

A place where no one would hear the hum. No one would see the light.

Roland took another sip, cock twitching at the thought.

He imagined bringing a young woman there. A casual excuse. A drink, perhaps. A promise of help with something. She'd step into the room, laugh at the odd towers standing opposite each other. She'd sit, unsuspecting, in the heart of the field.

And then 3.3 would do the rest.

Roland closed the notebook slowly, his pulse hammering.

He had lied to Sam. He had hidden the machine.

And now, he would find somewhere new.

Somewhere secret.

Somewhere made for sin.

The next morning, Roland drove out of town. At first, he told himself it was just for a drive, just to clear his head. But his eyes betrayed him, scanning every lay-by, every woodland track, every "To Let" sign on crumbling barns and disused shops.

Old warehouses. Remote cottages. Farm outbuildings. Each place sparked ideas. He imagined setting up the towers in a dusty loft, the hum of 3.3 filling the rafters. Or a basement flat, curtains drawn, where no one could hear the gasps and moans.

The possibilities quickened his pulse.

He stopped outside a derelict villa, its windows boarded, its garden overgrown. Perfect, he thought for a moment, until he noticed the developer's sign staked in the soil. Too obvious. Too likely to attract attention.

Further out, in the lanes beyond the bypass, he found an abandoned stable block. The roof sagged in places, but the walls were solid. Remote. Forgotten. The kind of place people passed without ever looking twice.

Roland parked and got out, walking the perimeter. No neighbours in sight. No lights. No signs of life.

He could see it already: the generator in one corner, the twin towers facing each other across the straw-strewn floor. A mattress dragged in, clean sheets. Candles, perhaps. He could invite anyone there under the right pretense — a favour, a drink, even just curiosity.

And once they were inside, once the field was on…

His cock thickened at the thought, shame and hunger twisting together.

By the time he drove home, Roland's mind was racing. He wasn't just hiding anymore. He was planning.

The bungalow had been too risky.

But the stable... the stable could be perfect.

All he needed now was the right girl.

Chapter Twelve
The Stable

Roland had always been cautious with money, but this… this was an investment.

When he called in at the estate agent, he played the role of the harmless pensioner. Sixty years old, soft voice, polite. He spoke about "a bit of hobby carpentry" and "a need for quiet space, out of Sam's way." He chuckled, mentioning neighbourly noise and how "a man sometimes needs his shed."

The agent barely blinked. Agricultural outbuildings were hard to let, and here was a man offering six months' rent upfront, no questions asked. They drew up the tenancy under "personal storage and hobby use." Roland signed with a steady hand, slipped the keys into his jacket, and drove away with his pulse hammering.

It was his.

The first visit nearly broke the fantasy. The stable reeked of damp hay and mice droppings. Dust clung to every beam. Weeds sprouted through the cracked threshold. If he brought anyone here in this state, they'd laugh—or worse, scream and run.

So he began the work.

Week one, he focused on the outside. He hired a local handyman—under the story that he wanted to use the place for woodworking—to patch the roof tiles, repaint the doors, and clear the weeds. A fresh coat of forest-green paint made the entrance look cared-for, almost quaint. He planted two tubs of lavender by the door, their scent masking the must of the interior. From the lane, it no longer looked abandoned. It looked… secret, tucked away, but safe.

Week two, he worked inside. He swept until his back ached, then hired a skip and cleared years of rubbish. He scrubbed the walls and floor with disinfectant until the air smelled sharp and clean. With curtains across the windows and a heavy drape behind the doors, no one could see in—or out.

Week three, he transformed. A Persian-style rug spread across the centre of the floor. A low bedframe and a firm double mattress, dressed with fresh cotton sheets, gave it an intimate softness. A set of dimmable lamps, hidden wiring, and a few candles turned the place from bare stone to something warmer, more private.

Finally, he added touches to make it disarming: a small bookshelf stacked with paperbacks, a table with two wine glasses and a bottle, even a heater tucked in the corner. He kept a spare blanket folded at the end of the bed. Nothing grand, nothing expensive—just enough to look inviting.

By the fourth week, Roland would stand in the doorway and smile. From the lane, the stable looked like a quiet hobby retreat, even a rustic studio. Step inside, and it whispered of something more.

And only he knew the truth.

Where the towers would stand. Where the hum of 3.3 would fill the air. Where the polite comfort of wine and small talk would dissolve into panting and cries.

His cock stirred at the thought, and he closed the door quickly, heart pounding.

The bungalow had been Sam's hunting ground. But the stable?

The stable was his theatre.

And soon, the curtains would rise.

✦ ✦ ✦

Chapter Thirteen
The Test

The stable smelled of lavender and wood polish now, not hay and damp. Roland stood at the doorway with the generator cradled in his arms, the two towers in a canvas bag at his feet.

It had taken all morning to drive them out discreetly, one trip at a time, hidden beneath blankets in the boot of his car. No one had seen. No one knew.

Now came the test.

He set the generator on the small table by the bed, running his hands over the familiar knobs and dials. It looked almost comical in this cleaned-up space, the hum of science against the softness of Persian rugs and cotton sheets. But Roland's stomach tightened as he laid the towers down—one at each end of the stable, aligned just so.

When everything was in place, he stepped back, breath held.

The switch clicked.

The generator gave its soft whine, then the deeper hum rolled out. The air shifted almost instantly, thick and subtle, like invisible silk stretching across the room.

Roland's skin prickled.

He turned the dial, steady, deliberate, until the numbers dropped into place: **3.3.**

The hum settled, low and steady, vibrating in his chest.

Roland closed his eyes.

Yes. It was here. The same as before.

His skin tingled. His cock began to swell without touch, a slow, insistent heat pooling low in his belly. His breath quickened, and for a moment he had to grip the edge of the table just to steady himself.

It worked.

Even here, far from the bungalow, far from Sam's curious eyes—the field was alive.

He walked the length of the stable, testing. Near the mattress, the pull was stronger, his cock twitching hard in his trousers. By the curtained doors, softer, but still there, humming through him like a pulse. He stepped outside into the lane, shut the doors, then opened them again and returned inside. The instant he crossed the threshold, the arousal came back sharp and urgent, as if the very air was charged.

He grinned despite himself, wiping sweat from his brow.

Perfect.

The 3.3 field was not bound to his bungalow. It wasn't about bricks or plaster. It was about the towers. The generator. The number.

Wherever he set them, the effect would be the same.

And that meant freedom.

Roland powered it down at last, panting, his cock hard and aching against his zipper. He didn't touch himself—not this time. This wasn't for indulgence. This was for certainty.

Now he knew.

The stable worked. The frequency held. The stage was ready.

Next time, it wouldn't be him alone in that field.

Next time, it would be her.

Whoever she was.

✦ ✦ ✦

Chapter Fourteen
The Cover Story

Roland sat at the small table inside the stable, notebook open, pen hovering. The place was ready. Cleaned, painted, softened with rugs and sheets. From the outside, it looked rustic and safe. Inside, it was secretive, perfect.

But perfection meant nothing if he couldn't get anyone through the door.

He tapped the pen against the page, staring at the blank lines.

'Why would a young woman come here?'

He wrote the question at the top, underlined it twice, and began to list answers.

1. Photography.

Everyone wanted pictures these days. Portraits for portfolios, social media, dating apps. He could buy a decent camera, set up a backdrop, string a light or two. "Free portraits" — harmless, friendly, nothing threatening. Students would leap at it. They'd bring their own clothes, pose willingly. And once they were inside, once the hum of 3.3 filled the air...

Roland closed his eyes, imagining the scene: a girl in her twenties, smiling nervously at first, then shifting, nipples stiff beneath her top, cheeks flushed. Her smile would falter into parted lips, her laughter replaced with moans.

He gripped the pen tighter, forcing himself back to the page.

2. Wellness.
The word was everywhere. Wellness, mindfulness, self-care. He could spin the stable as a "quiet retreat space." Offer free meditation sessions, breathing exercises, or even "experimental relaxation frequencies." Women flocked to that sort of thing. They'd expect nothing but calm and safety.

And safety was the perfect disguise.

He pictured yoga mats lined across the rug, girls in leggings stretching, then freezing as the hum worked through them. Their bodies softening, sighs slipping from their mouths. A meditation turning into a moan.

His cock stirred, and he shifted uncomfortably in the chair.

3. Work.
The simplest of all: a job. He could say he needed help clearing boxes, painting walls, sorting books. Cash in hand, quick and easy. Students, single mums, waitresses with tight budgets — they'd say yes without thinking.

And once they stepped inside, once they breathed the field...

He shook his head, scribbling a line through it. Too plain. Too obvious. Work implied sweat, effort, something they could leave quickly. It didn't have the allure he wanted.

Roland leaned back, pen against his lips. The ideas weren't bad. Photography had promise. Wellness too, though it risked attracting the wrong kind of attention if he wasn't careful.

He needed something simple, disarming, and believable. Something that would make a girl step inside without suspicion.

Not sex. Never sex. Not openly. That's the trick. The promise has to be innocent.

He scrawled the words across the page.

The hum of the stable felt louder in his head, though the machine wasn't even on. He pictured the towers standing ready, invisible silk stretched between them, waiting.

It was all so close.

Now he just had to choose the bait.

And once he had that...

The trap would be perfect.

Chapter Fifteen
The Leaflets

Roland had made up his mind: photography was the perfect cover. It gave him a reason to invite women into the stable, one at a time, without raising eyebrows. Better yet, it gave them a reason to want to come.

He sat at his kitchen table, laptop open, the glow of the screen reflecting in his glasses. The last time he had used any design software was years ago, but he managed to piece something together. A simple border, a faint logo he copied from the internet, neat text in a soft font. Nothing flashy. Nothing intimidating.

At the top, he typed:

Free Portrait Photography – Students & Young Adults Welcome

Beneath that, in smaller letters:

Local retired hobbyist with a quiet countryside studio is offering free portrait sessions. Receive your own prints to keep. Ideal for creative portfolios, social media, or simply a gift for yourself.

He paused, then added:

One or two at a time only. Casual, friendly, and safe environment.

The word safe made him smirk. True enough, in its own twisted way.

The leaflet slowly took shape. He chose soft pastel colours, easy on the eye. He added a stock image of a smiling young woman, hair blowing slightly, looking carefree.

At the bottom, he left a simple contact: a new email address he had set up, untraceable to his main accounts. Nothing personal. Nothing to tie back to Roland the man, only Roland the "retired hobbyist."

When he hit print, the inkjet whirred to life. One by one, the pages slid out, warm and smelling faintly chemical. Roland held the first copy in his hand, smoothing the edge.

It looked innocent. Harmless. Almost wholesome.

No one would suspect a thing.

He stacked the leaflets in neat piles, already imagining where he'd leave them: cafés near the university, noticeboards at community centres, maybe even slipped into the library. Anywhere young women might linger, bored, open to something new.

The fantasy bled into his thoughts again. He pictured a girl picking one up, smiling at the offer, thinking it was nothing more than a quirky opportunity. She'd send him an email, they'd exchange a few polite words, and soon enough she'd be standing in the stable doorway, nervous but curious.

He felt his cock swell at the thought. He pushed the fantasy down, focusing instead on the paper in his hands.

This wasn't indulgence. Not yet. This was preparation.

Roland laid the leaflets out to dry, lined like soldiers across the table. The hum of the machine seemed to echo in his memory, though it sat silent in the stable a couple of miles away.

By tomorrow, these leaflets would start appearing around town. By the end of the week, perhaps his inbox would not be empty.

And then the real work would begin.

✦ ✦ ✦

Chapter Sixteen
The Encounter

Roland tucked the stack of leaflets into a plain brown envelope, locked his front door, and stepped into the soft morning air. The world felt crisp with possibility. By the end of the day, the leaflets would be pinned to noticeboards and café walls. By the end of the week, his inbox might have the first response.

He adjusted his jacket, humming quietly — until he heard her voice.

"Morning, Roland."

Sam.

She was in her garden, crouched by the flowerbed, trowel in hand. Her hair was tied up, a loose strand falling against her cheek. She looked relaxed, casual, but her eyes flicked up at him with that sharpness he knew too well.

Roland forced a smile. "Morning, Sam. Lovely day for it."

"Mm," she said, digging the soil. "Out for a walk?"

"Just errands," he replied quickly. He shifted the envelope under his arm, careful not to let the papers show.

Sam tilted her head. "Funny. You seem cheerier than usual."

Roland chuckled softly. "Getting on with things, that's all. Feels good to have less on my plate."

Her gaze lingered. "You mean the machine?"

His heart gave a sudden thump, but he kept his face smooth. "Yes. That's gone now. Sold it a few weeks ago. Overseas buyer, I told you."

She straightened slowly, brushing soil from her gloves. "Still can't believe you did that. Could've made a fortune, Roland."

He shrugged, feigning ease. "Money's not everything. Peace of mind's worth more at my age."

Sam studied him, lips twitching in a half-smile. "You don't fool me, you know. You're hiding something."

Roland's stomach tightened, but he let out a dry laugh. "At sixty, we're all hiding something. Usually back pain."

Her eyes narrowed, then softened as she gave a mock roll of her eyes. "You're hopeless."

She bent back to her flowers, letting the conversation drop.

Roland exhaled slowly, relief washing through him. He turned, heading down the lane, envelope clutched tight under his arm.

As he walked, his mind replayed the exchange. Sam didn't believe him — not really. But she couldn't prove anything. That was the key.

And once the leaflets were out, once his first visitor arrived at the stable, Sam would be nothing more than a memory of temptation past.

He smiled faintly, quickening his step.

The stage was set.

The actors would come.

And none of them would ever suspect the truth until they were already inside the field.

The bus into town was half full. Roland sat near the window, envelope on his lap, eyes flicking across shopfronts as the streets rolled past. Each one was a potential hunting ground.

His first stop was a café near the university. It was bright, busy, and filled with chatter. Students hunched over laptops, young women laughing over lattes. Roland's mouth went dry as he stepped inside.

At the counter, he ordered tea and a slice of carrot cake, forcing a genial smile. "Lovely place you've got here," he told the barista, a young man with a pierced eyebrow. When his plate arrived, he slid one of the leaflets across. "I do a bit of amateur photography. Just portraits, nothing professional. Would it be alright if I left a few on your noticeboard?"

The barista glanced at it, shrugged, and nodded towards the corkboard by the door. "As long as you pin them yourself."

"Much obliged," Roland said warmly.

He sipped his tea slowly, waiting for the moment to tack the leaflet neatly between a flyer for guitar lessons and a poster for yoga classes. When he stepped back, it looked perfectly ordinary. Invisible among the clutter.

Next, he tried the independent bookshop on the corner. The smell of paper and ink clung to the air, and a girl with dyed red hair stacked paperbacks behind the counter. Roland browsed for a while, careful not to seem rushed, before approaching with his leaflet folded in hand.

"Afternoon," he said softly. "I'm a retired hobbyist photographer. I wondered if you keep a community board?"

She looked him over quickly, then nodded towards the back wall. "Pin it yourself. Just don't cover the events."

Roland thanked her and placed two copies among flyers for poetry readings and craft fairs. Again, harmless. Invisible.

The library was next. Quieter, more formal. Here he spoke to the woman at the desk — middle-aged, glasses, polite but brisk. He explained his "small project," how he "enjoyed giving students free portraits as practice." She hesitated a moment, then handed him a pin. "Community board's near the entrance. Keep it tidy."

Roland smiled gratefully. "Of course."

He pinned three leaflets in a neat row. From the corner of his eye, he saw a girl in leggings and trainers glance at the board before leaving. His pulse quickened.

By the time Roland made his way home, the envelope was lighter. Copies of his innocent little advert now hung in cafés, bookshops, libraries, and community spaces across town. To anyone else, they were just another flyer.

But to him, each one was bait.

Each one was a door.

And sooner or later, someone would walk through.

◆ ◆ ◆

Chapter Seventeen
The Rehearsal

Roland locked up his bungalow just after dusk, slid behind the wheel of his ageing saloon, and drove the winding road out of town. The headlights swept across hedgerows and empty fields until, at last, the shape of the old stable appeared, hunched and waiting in the dark.

The air was sharp, biting against his cheeks, and he drew his coat tighter around him. He'd decided it was time to spend a full night out there — not just to test the cold, but to stage, in his mind, the scene he was so carefully constructing.

When he opened the stable door, a breath of chill air greeted him. The rugs he'd laid helped a little, but not enough. If he was going to lure anyone here, he needed to make it inviting. The heater would be essential, perhaps two. Nothing that buzzed or looked industrial, just small, safe, domestic warmth.

He lit a lamp, the golden glow softening the corners. He pulled a chair into the centre of the room and sat, facing the blank wall where he imagined hanging a backdrop for his "studio."

He closed his eyes and pictured it.

A knock at the door. A young woman's voice: *"Hello? I saw your flyer."*

He stood, walked to the door, and opened it to the empty night. "Welcome, welcome. Thank you for coming. It's nothing professional, you understand, just a bit of fun for practice." His own voice echoed strangely in the bare space.

He ushered the invisible guest inside, gesturing toward the rug. "Make yourself comfortable. It's warmer than it looks."

He paused, listening to the silence.

And then, imagining the voice again: *"It's a bit... different. A stable?"*

Roland smiled faintly to himself, answering aloud. "Ah, yes, it was all I could get for the price. But it's quiet, private. You'll see, the pictures turn out rather well."

He shifted, lowering himself back into the chair. The cold seeped through his trousers, making him shiver. He made a note in his pocket diary: *Extra heater. More rugs. Cushions.*

Back to the rehearsal.

He pictured the girl again, pulling a strand of hair behind her ear, uncertain but not frightened. He imagined offering tea from a flask, showing her the camera, making her laugh with some gentle, harmless comment.

And then the moment of truth: the machine. How would he explain it?

"Don't worry about the towers," he muttered to himself. "They're part of the lighting set-up. Completely harmless."

He tilted his head, testing the words. Not perfect, but close enough.

And if she frowned? If she felt something was wrong?

Roland stood abruptly, pacing. "If anyone asks to leave, you let them go. Straight away. That way there's no story to tell, no trouble later." He wrote it down: *Rule One — Never resist. If they want to leave, let them.*

But in his gut, he felt the rule might never be tested. Because once the field began to hum at 3.3, once the resonance touched her nerves and blood and breath… leaving wouldn't be on her mind at all.

He sat back down, the stable quiet around him. He stayed like that for hours — staging, rehearsing, refining. Until finally he curled on the makeshift bedroll, coat pulled tight, and closed his eyes. The cold gnawed at him, but he barely noticed.

In his dreams, the stable was already alive with soft laughter, flushed skin, and the hum of a frequency no one else understood.

✦ ✦ ✦

Chapter Eighteen
The First Replies

Two weeks had passed.

Roland had almost given up checking the email account he'd set up for the leaflets. Each night he logged in with a flicker of hope, only to find the inbox stubbornly empty. The disappointment gnawed at him, especially after all his careful work. The stable stood ready, silent, like a stage waiting for an audience that never arrived.

Until tonight.

Roland clicked refresh and froze. Two new messages.

His throat went dry. His hand hovered over the mouse as though opening them too quickly might scare them away. He forced himself to breathe slowly, steadying the tremor of excitement running through him.

The first email was short, typed without much punctuation:

Hi, I saw your flyer in the café. I'm a student, just looking for some nice photos for my profile. Could I come by sometime this week? – Sophie

Roland read it three times. Sophie. A name, a hook, a possibility. She hadn't asked about money, hadn't questioned the address. Just trust. Just interest.

His cock stirred at the thought, and he pushed the fantasy down, focusing on the second message.

This one was longer, more cautious:

Hello. I picked up your leaflet at the library. I'm not sure if I'm what you're looking for, but I'd love to have a few portraits taken. I've never done anything like this before, but it sounds fun. Could you tell me a bit more about your set-up? – Emily

Roland sat back in his chair, heart thudding. Two women. Two doors opening at once. Sophie sounded impulsive, almost careless — a student who wanted something quick, easy, harmless. Emily was different: hesitant, testing the waters, needing reassurance.

He smiled faintly. He could handle both.

He tapped the desk with his pen, weighing his response. He had to sound friendly, safe, reliable. Nothing that would put them off.

For Sophie, he drafted:

Hello Sophie, thank you for your interest. Yes, I can do a session this week. It's very relaxed, nothing formal. I have a small studio just outside town where it's quiet and private. Would you be free one afternoon?

For Emily, he softened his tone further:

Hello Emily, thank you for writing. There's no requirement at all — it's just practice for me, and I give you the prints for free. I've set up a small studio space in an old converted stable. It's cosy and quiet. Nothing professional, just for fun. If you'd like, you're welcome to come and have a look first, and if you don't feel comfortable, there's no obligation to stay.

He read them back, nodding. They struck the right balance: honest enough to reassure, vague enough to conceal.

Leaning back, Roland let his mind wander. He pictured Sophie — bold, careless, walking into the stable without hesitation. He saw Emily — cautious, reserved, but softening as he smiled, as he poured her tea, as the field began to hum.

He imagined them both, separate nights, different flavours of innocence about to turn into something raw and unrestrained.

The stable would no longer be silent.

The stage was finally set.

And the actors were on their way.

✦ ✦ ✦

Chapter Nineteen
Sophie

Roland wiped his palms on his trousers as the car headlights swept up the lane. A small hatchback pulled into view, music thudding faintly from inside before the engine cut off.

She climbed out, stumbling slightly on her heels. Sophie. Twenty-something, brunette, skinny jeans, a crop top under an oversized jacket. Pretty, though her eyes were glassy, her movements loose.

"Hi!" she called brightly, almost too loudly. "You're Roland?"

"That's right," he said, forcing calm into his voice. "Thank you for coming."

She giggled, swaying as she pulled a tote bag from the passenger seat. "No worries. Thought it sounded fun."

Inside the stable, Roland gestured to the chair he'd set up, a plain backdrop hanging behind it. "We'll just take a few shots, nothing complicated."

Sophie nodded, but her eyes darted everywhere, restless. "Cool space. Bit weird, though." She laughed again, half-snorting.

Roland studied her. There was something off — her pupils wide, her words too fast. High on something.

Pills? Cocaine? He couldn't tell. A stab of doubt went through him. 'Is this safe?'

But then he remembered the machine. This was the perfect chance to test. Not with 3.3 — not yet. He wanted to know how other frequencies behaved, how different states of mind reacted.

He busied himself with the camera, then casually flicked the generator on. The towers glowed faintly, the hum settling at 14.6.

At first, Sophie only tilted her head. "What's that?"

"Lighting," Roland lied smoothly. "You won't notice it."

But then her breath hitched. She clutched at her stomach, then her temples.

"Whoa. Oh my god. What the fuck—"

Her eyes widened in panic. She staggered back from the chair, hands shaking. "I feel—oh god, I feel like I'm having a fit—"

Roland's chest tightened. "It's fine. You're fine. Sit down—"

But she was already fumbling for her bag, voice trembling. "I—I can't. I'm sorry, I need to go, I'm sorry—"

And just like that, she bolted. The door slammed. Outside, her car engine roared to life, headlights sweeping wildly before she sped down the lane, tyres spitting gravel.

Silence.

Roland stood frozen, the low hum still vibrating through the stable. His heart hammered. That hadn't been arousal. That had been terror.

Slowly, he switched off the generator.

He sat down, running a hand over his face. What had gone wrong? Was it the frequency? Or was it her state of mind? Drugs. Alcohol. Something in her system.

He pulled out his notebook, writing quickly, hand shaking.

Tested frequency 14.6. Result: subject panicked, described feeling like seizure. Left abruptly. Hypothesis: intoxication may conflict with field. Possible rule — never combine with drugs or alcohol.

He stared at the words.

This wasn't just about arousal. The field was unpredictable. Dangerous, even.

But his cock still stirred faintly at the memory of Sophie's body, the way she had looked in his chair, laughing, unsteady. He swallowed hard, guilt and hunger tangling together.

He knew one thing for certain: 14.6 wasn't the answer.

But 3.3 still waited.

✦ ✦ ✦

Chapter Twenty

Emily

Roland stared at the glow of his laptop long after Sophie's car had vanished from memory. He'd replayed her panic a dozen times, analysing every twitch, every gasp. The field at 14.6 hadn't aroused her — it had scrambled her. Drugs, he decided. Her body simply wasn't stable enough to handle resonance.

That had to be it.

He opened his notebook, underlined the words *No drugs. No alcohol.* three times, then circled them. A new rule. A vital one.

His inbox still contained Emily's cautious message. He hovered over it, debating. She was different from Sophie — slower, more thoughtful, nervous even. If he frightened her, she would vanish. But if he handled it right... she might stay.

Later that night, as he lay in bed, Roland let his imagination drift. Emily walking into the stable, cautious eyes scanning the space. Emily sitting in the chair, hands folded, waiting. And then the low hum of 3.3 filling the air, subtle as a whisper.He pictured her thighs shifting, her breath catching, her lips parting. Not panic. Not fear. Just arousal. Deep, unstoppable arousal.

Roland stroked himself slowly in the dark, breath shallow. This time it would work. This time, everything would unfold the way he had dreamed.

He closed his eyes and whispered to the night: "Emily."

The lane to the stable was quiet, hedgerows heavy with dusk, when Roland saw headlights sweep across the gravel. His chest tightened as the car rolled to a stop. She'd come.

Emily stepped out, closing the door with careful hands. She was younger than he had imagined from her email — mid-twenties, perhaps. Shoulder-length blonde hair, faintly curled, a simple navy jumper that clung softly to her chest, and jeans tucked into ankle boots. A canvas tote hung from her shoulder. She looked practical, neat, with the kind of understated beauty that revealed itself the longer you stared.

"Hi," she said, her voice gentle but uncertain.

Roland smiled warmly, forcing steadiness into his tone. "Emily. Thank you for coming. I know it's a bit out of the way."

She gave a quick smile. "That's okay. It's quiet, isn't it?"

"Very," Roland replied, stepping aside to let her in. "Please, make yourself comfortable. Tea?"

She accepted the flask cup he poured, sipping gratefully as her eyes roamed the stable. The rugs, the backdrop he'd hung, the camera on its tripod — all carefully placed to look harmless.

"It's… nice," she said, though the hesitation in her voice was clear.

"Nothing professional," Roland assured her. "Just a hobby. We'll start very simple. Sit where you feel comfortable, and I'll just take a few shots to see how the light falls."

Emily nodded, set her tote aside, and sat in the wooden chair before the backdrop. She folded her hands in her lap, posture straight, like a school photograph.

"Perfect," Roland said softly, raising the camera. "Just look at me."

The shutter clicked. Emily blinked at the sound, then relaxed slightly. Another shot, then another.

"Now, lean back a little. That's it. Tilt your head— good. Try a smile."

A small smile flickered across her lips. The lens caught it, gentle and unguarded.

Roland kept his voice calm, steady. "Wonderful. Now look away, as if you're thinking of something. Yes. Hold that."

The sequence flowed slowly, naturally. She crossed one leg over the other, toyed with a strand of hair, tilted her chin down. The shutter captured each movement.

Emily gave a small laugh at one point. "I feel silly."

"That's perfectly normal," Roland replied smoothly. "You're doing brilliantly. Just be yourself."

He stepped back, lowering the camera for a moment. His eyes took her in properly now — the soft curve of her breasts beneath the jumper, the faint rise and fall of her chest as she breathed, the way her jeans hugged her thighs. Nothing provocative, nothing staged. Just her. Real, present.

And soon, he thought, the machine would coax out what lay beneath.

But not yet. For now, the moment was fragile, delicate. He let her shift into another pose, resting her chin on her hand, eyes thoughtful. He photographed the curve of her cheek, the softness of her lips.

The stable felt quiet, safe, almost too safe.

Roland knew the stillness wouldn't last.

Emily brushed a strand of hair from her face, cheeks colouring faintly. "It's warm in here with the lamp on," she murmured.

Roland gestured gently. "Feel free to take off your jumper if you'd like. Whatever makes you comfortable."

She hesitated, then tugged it over her head, folding it neatly on the chair beside her. Underneath, she wore a crisp white blouse, the fabric fitted close to her frame. The buttons strained ever so slightly across her chest, hinting at the swell of her breasts.

Roland raised the camera, his breath slow. "Lovely. Just sit as you are."

The shutter clicked softly. Emily shifted, placing her hands on her knees, posture relaxed now.

"Turn a little to your left… perfect. Now glance back towards me."

She obeyed, her blouse catching the lamplight, the faint outline of her bra just visible beneath the thin fabric. Her jeans were snug, the denim clinging tightly along her thighs. As she shifted again, crossing her legs, Roland caught a glimpse — the faint cleft pressing through the seam of her jeans. A flash of *camel toe*, unintentional, natural, achingly real.

He swallowed, steadying the camera. "Excellent. Just like that. Hold it for me."

Emily gave a small laugh. "You make it sound serious."

"Not serious," Roland said, lowering the camera slightly to hide the tremor in his voice. "Just… beautiful."

She tilted her head, amused, but didn't object. Instead, she leaned back in the chair, one hand resting lightly on her hip. The blouse stretched across her torso, the top button gaping open just enough to tease.

Roland took another shot, then another, careful not to let his hunger show. Each click of the shutter felt like a pulse, like time edging closer to the moment he had been waiting for.

But not yet. Not quite yet.

The stage was still being set.

Roland adjusted the camera, pretending to fiddle with the focus. "Let's try a little variation," he said, his voice calm though his heart thudded.

He reached behind him, flicking the generator to life. The hum filled the stable, soft and low, set deliberately to 14.6.

Emily blinked, shifting in her chair. Her posture straightened, then loosened again, a curious relaxation spreading across her limbs. She brushed her blouse down over her waist, then leaned forward a little, smiling in a way that seemed freer than before.

"Like this?" she asked, tilting her head, chin high.

"Yes," Roland murmured, the camera clicking.

She laughed softly, then shifted her legs apart just slightly, one knee angled outwards. The seam of her jeans stretched tight, pulling at the crotch, the faint curve of her cleft pressed plainly through the denim.

Roland swallowed hard, fighting the heat rising in him.

Emily's eyes glittered faintly in the lamplight. "Maybe... something less stiff. More playful." She leaned back, tugging her blouse tighter across her chest, the fabric straining.

"Perfect," Roland whispered, his cock stiffening as he pressed the shutter again.

Her movements grew bolder with each pose. She ran her fingers slowly through her hair, letting it fall about her shoulders. She stood, resting one hand against the backdrop pole, her hips tilted, blouse riding just enough to show a sliver of bare stomach.

"Mm… feels different now," she murmured, half to herself.

Roland didn't answer, only captured the curve of her waist, the faint arch of her back.

Finally, Emily turned, biting her lip. "Can I ask you something?"

"Of course."

She stepped closer to the chair, leaning against it, her blouse gaping open just slightly. Her eyes held his, curious, daring.

"Would you mind," she said slowly, "if we… tried some more… erotic photos?"

Her cheeks coloured, but her smile lingered. "Just for me. Something private. I've never done it before."

Roland's throat tightened. His cock strained painfully against his trousers.

But he kept his voice steady. "Well...If. If, that's what you'd like."

Emily nodded, already unbuttoning the next clasp of her blouse with trembling fingers.

Emily drew in a breath and popped the next button of her blouse. The fabric parted just enough to reveal the lacy trim of a pale bra beneath. She gave a nervous laugh, brushing a strand of hair from her eyes.

"I feel ridiculous," she said, though her voice carried more excitement than embarrassment.

Roland steadied the camera. "Not ridiculous at all. You look... striking."

The shutter clicked.

Emily adjusted her stance, tilting her hips, arching her back slightly. The blouse fell looser with each subtle shift.

"Maybe like this?" She pressed one hand to her thigh, glancing over her shoulder with a playful smile.

"Yes," Roland breathed. "Hold that."

Another button slipped free. Her blouse gaped wider now, the swell of her breasts framed perfectly by the lace.

Roland's pulse thundered. His cock throbbed against his trousers, but still he held the role of calm photographer.

Emily leaned against the chair, head tilted, lips parted. "You know… I didn't think I'd enjoy this," she admitted. "But I feel… different. Lighter. Like I want to…" She trailed off, laughing again, a low, throaty sound.

She placed her hands on her hips, slowly sliding her thumbs beneath the waistband of her jeans, tugging them down just a fraction. The denim hugged tighter across her crotch, the seam cutting against her cleft, her camel toe outlined with glaring clarity.

Roland snapped the shot, his hand slightly trembling.

Emily giggled, looking down at herself. "That's a bit naughty, isn't it?"

"Only if you want it to be," Roland murmured, his voice hoarse.

She looked up at him then, eyes glinting with mischief. She tugged the jeans down another inch, baring a hint of skin at her hips, the lace of matching underwear peeking above the denim.

"Maybe one more button…" she whispered, undoing it slowly. Her blouse now hung open to the waist, her bra fully revealed, nipples stiff beneath the sheer lace.

She posed deliberately, arching her back, lifting her hair with both hands so that her chest thrust forward. "Take it now," she teased, voice soft but sure.

Roland obeyed, the shutter clicking, his breath ragged.

He could feel the urge clawing at him, to step forward, to drop the camera, to touch. But he stayed rooted, trembling with restraint, watching as Emily experimented with her own daring.

This wasn't all abandonment — not yet. She wasn't lost to the field. She was playing. Testing herself. Testing him.

And Roland, every nerve alive with arousal, knew he was only seeing the beginning.

Emily's fingers hovered at her bra strap, her eyes flicking up to Roland with a half-smile. "Should we… try one without?"

Roland's throat tightened. "If you're comfortable."

She laughed softly. "I think I am."

Her hands moved quickly then, unclasping the hooks, slipping the straps from her shoulders. She let the bra fall to the chair, her breasts spilling free, firm and round, nipples already stiff in the cool air.

Roland swallowed hard, lifting the camera again. "Beautiful," he murmured, and the shutter clicked.

Emily tilted her head back, hair falling loose, one hand sliding up to cup herself, thumb grazing a nipple. She laughed again — not embarrassed, but playful, testing her own boldness.

"This is mad," she said between giggles. "I never thought I'd be standing topless in some converted stable, letting a stranger take photos of me."

"Not mad," Roland replied quietly. "Just... honest."

The words seemed to land. She shifted, arching her back, lifting both hands behind her head so her breasts thrust forward. The flash captured the curve of her skin, the flush of her chest.

Roland's cock strained painfully against his trousers. His hand itched to drop the camera, to touch, to take — but he held himself firm. This was not the moment. Not yet.

For half an hour, Emily moved through pose after pose, each one more daring than the last. Kneeling on the rug, pressing her arms together to accentuate her cleavage. Standing with her jeans tugged low, teasing the waistband of her underwear. Turning her body side-on, one nipple silhouetted in the lamplight.

She wasn't lost, not fully — but she was freer, bolder, glowing with a confidence she hadn't walked in with.

And then, as her breathing grew heavier and her laughter softened into small sighs, Roland knew it was time.

He lowered the camera, flicked the generator off. The hum died instantly.

Emily blinked, swaying slightly, then let out a long breath. "Wow," she whispered.

Roland gave a gentle nod, hiding the quake in his chest. "You were wonderful."

Emily buttoned her blouse slowly, still flushed, but calm now. She gathered her jumper over one arm and glanced at the camera resting in Roland's hands.

"You'll... send me the photos?" she asked softly.

Roland nodded, steadying his voice. "Yes. I'll go through them tonight, make a small selection. I'll email them to you within a couple of days."

Her smile spread, easy and genuine. "Good. I'd like that."

She moved to the door, pausing with one hand on the frame. "I really did enjoy it, Roland. It felt... freeing. Like finding a part of myself I didn't know was there."

He inclined his head, keeping his tone measured though his cock still pulsed painfully. "You were wonderful to work with, Emily."

Her eyes lingered on his for a moment, as though she wanted to say more, then she slipped out into the cool night.

When the sound of her car faded into the distance, Roland stood in the silence of the stable, camera heavy in his hands, the scent of her skin still hanging in the air.

She would have her photographs. Proof of her playfulness. A reminder of the night.

And he would have the images, too — but more than that, he had confirmation of what the machine could coax from even the most reserved woman.

14.6 had brought out confidence.

3.3 would bring out everything else.

Chapter Twenty One

Roland sat at his desk the following evening, the glow of his monitor lighting the room as Emily's photographs scrolled across the screen.

He clicked slowly through the hundreds of shots, pausing on each one.

Emily smiling in her blouse, innocent. Emily leaning back, hair tumbling. Emily parting her lips in a playful sigh. Emily topless, nipples stiff, her hand cupping herself with almost unconscious ease.

He marked a handful, no more than twelve. Enough to feel like a natural selection, not an indulgence. Not the ones where her jeans rode too low or her nipples stood out brazenly. No — those he kept for himself.

The set he chose for Emily were carefully balanced: playful, relaxed, teasing… just enough to remind her of the heat in her chest, the laughter on her lips. Just enough to whisper 'you were braver than you thought you could be.'

He imagined her opening the email at home, her fingers scrolling through the images. The way her stomach would twist as she saw herself smiling, stripped to the waist, not ashamed but radiant.

And he knew — he knew — the thought would creep in: 'I want to feel that again.'

She wouldn't be able to dismiss it as a silly moment. She would have the evidence now, sitting in her inbox, undeniable and hers alone.

Roland leaned back, the ache in his trousers unbearable but exquisite. He didn't touch himself. He didn't need to. The real release was in the control, in knowing she was already half-his without even realising it.

With one final click, he attached the chosen photos to an email, typed a short, polite message, and hit - send.

The rest, the hungrier shots, the ones that showed her nipples straining and her jeans tugged so low the lace of her underwear peeked through — those he kept locked in a private folder.

Her photos would tease her. His photos would feed him.

And in both their minds, the question would burn the same:

'Would she want it again?'

He thought of the hum at 14.6, the way it had loosened her laugh, straightened her back, then coaxed her into unfastening her blouse with trembling hands. He remembered the way she giggled, calling herself "ridiculous" — when she was already topless, teasing the camera with a confidence she hadn't walked in with.

And all the while, he had been in control.

At any moment he could have leaned over, adjusted the dial to 3.3, and the game would have been over. Emily would have slipped from playful daring into pure, irresistible need. She would have spread her legs, touched herself, begged for more — and he could have taken her, there and then, without question.

That knowledge sent a deeper thrill through him than anything else. He hadn't needed to fuck her. He hadn't even needed to touch her. What aroused him was the power. The certainty that he held the key to her desire, and that he alone could decide when it turned.

He leaned back in his chair, exhaling through his nose, cock straining painfully against his trousers.

It was a revelation: he didn't need to rush. He didn't need to throw himself at every opportunity. He could let them tease him. He could let them strip, laugh, and play under 14.6, pretending it was just a bit of fun. He could watch, drink it in, feel his arousal coil tighter and tighter…

…because he knew. At any second, he could turn the dial.

That was his pleasure. That was his control.

Roland closed the folder, shutting off the monitor. His cock was throbbing, his body tight with hunger, but he didn't touch himself. The ache was almost sweeter than release.

Emily had given him proof. Not just of the machine's effect, but of his own power.

And now, he thought as he sat in the dark, there would be others.

Women who would walk into his stable, smiling, laughing, thinking it was only a game.

And he — calm, patient, utterly in control — would decide how far it went.

Chapter Twenty Two

Roland sat in the stable again, the faint smell of wood polish still clinging to the air from his last tidy-up. His laptop glowed in front of him, Emily's folder open on the screen.

He scrolled slowly through the images.

Emily smiling in her blouse. Emily unbuttoned, chest rising and falling, a flicker of mischief in her eyes. Emily topless, her nipples stiff, her hair cascading down her shoulders.

He leaned closer, chin resting in his palm. They were good. Better than good. Even without the knowledge of the machine's influence, they looked natural, sensual, almost professional. There was no stiffness, no forced poses. She looked comfortable, radiant, as if the idea of undressing for a stranger's camera had always been her secret delight.

But he knew the truth. Without the hum of 14.6, she would never have undone a single button.

That was the question clawing at him now. Could he use these photographs? If another young woman came to the stable, if she hesitated at the idea of posing, could he show her these and say: 'Look, this is what others have done. You'll enjoy it too.'

Or would it break the spell? Would they see through it?

Roland tapped the side of the table with his fingers, a smile tugging faintly at his lips.

He didn't need to show these photos to anyone. That was the beauty of it.

Emily had no idea why she'd stripped. Why she'd laughed, posed, revealed herself so boldly. To her, it had simply felt natural — like discovering a hidden part of herself. She would remember it that way forever.

And any woman who came after her would feel the same.

The machine was all he needed. A hum at 14.6 to coax playfulness. A shift to 3.3 to strip away every last boundary. Their resolve, their doubts, their hesitation — gone in an instant.

No photos required. No persuasion.

Roland sat back, his cock stiff against his trousers, eyes half-closed with pleasure.

All he had to do was wait. Bring them in. Let the hum do its work.

He alone held the key.

The fantasy was intoxicating.

Roland shut the laptop with a snap, sitting back in the chair. His breath came slow, deliberate.

It wasn't about blackmail. It wasn't about deceit. The machine gave them freedom they didn't even know they wanted. Emily was proof of that.

Still, he couldn't shake the question twisting inside him:

Were the photographs convincing enough to draw another woman in?

And was he bold enough to try?

Chapter Twenty Three

A week had crawled by. Roland had checked his inbox each evening with a mixture of hope and dread, telling himself it didn't matter, that Emily was just one encounter, an experiment. But the silence had gnawed at him all the same.

On the seventh night, he refreshed his emails and saw the unread count flicker to two.

His chest tightened.

The first message bore a name he didn't recognise. A young woman — polite, tentative — asking if his "studio sessions" were still available, saying she'd seen the leaflet in a café and liked the idea of something different. Her words were careful, but Roland could read the curiosity between each line.

The second message stopped him cold.

Emily.

Her subject line was simple: *Thank you.*

He opened it, pulse thundering.

Roland, I wanted to say how much I enjoyed last week. The photos you sent were better than I ever expected — I can't stop looking at them. I feel more confident just knowing they exist. I would love to do another shoot, and this time I'd like to pay you properly. Please let me know if that would be all right.

Roland leaned back in his chair, a slow smile tugging at the corners of his mouth.

She wanted to pay. Not only return, but invest. It was no longer a favour or a curiosity — it was something she valued, something she believed had unlocked part of herself.

His cock stiffened at the thought. Emily, topless in his stable, laughing as she unbuttoned her blouse. Emily, flushing but unashamed as she saw her photographs. Emily, now hungry enough to come back on her own terms.

And beyond her, another woman — nameless for now, but already knocking on the door.

The stable was working. The machine was working. His plan was beginning to take root.

Roland closed his laptop with deliberate care, savouring the heat coursing through him.

Two women waiting. Two paths opening before him.

And the hum of the generator already alive in his mind.

Roland opened the first message again — the new woman. Her name was Anna. The words were brief, a little shy, but there was a spark of curiosity in them that told him she had read his leaflet more than once before writing.

He began to type:

Hello Anna,
Thank you for your interest. Yes, the sessions are available. The

pace is entirely up to you — some people start with simple portraits, others experiment with style once they feel comfortable. Let me know when you feel ready and we'll arrange a time that suits you.

He read it back twice before hitting send. Friendly. Polite. Non-committal. It gave her control, or at least the illusion of it.

Then he turned to Emily's message.

This was different.

She wanted to pay. That small detail had gnawed at him since he'd read it. Money changed the shape of things. Money suggested business, transactions, expectation. And yet, it also proved something undeniable: she valued what had happened. She wanted more.

He sat back in his chair, fingers steepled, staring at the glow of the monitor.

How much should he ask for? A token sum — enough to make her feel she was supporting him? Or should he refuse and call it a hobby again, keeping her tethered by generosity?

If he accepted payment, he became the "photographer" in her mind. But if he refused, he remained the indulgence, the secret thrill she was lucky to stumble upon.

Roland's cock stirred at the thought. He liked the latter. He liked the power of giving freely, of making her feel chosen. That way, she wouldn't just be a client. She would be his.

He began typing.

Hello Emily,
I'm so glad to hear you enjoyed the shoot and that the photos gave you confidence. That was always my hope. There's no need for payment — I see this as a hobby, something I enjoy doing, and you were a delight to work with. I'd be more than happy to arrange another session whenever you'd like.

He paused, fingers hovering, then added one final line:

And thank you, truly, for your trust.

He hit send.

The decision pleased him. She would come again, not as a customer but as a woman eager for more of what she couldn't quite explain.

And when she stepped back into the stable, blouse buttoned, smiling nervously, he would have the power to decide whether it was 14.6 again… or 3.3

✦ ✦ ✦

Chapter Twenty Four

The reply came sooner than Roland expected.

Anna — the name was shorter than in her first email, clipped and polite — wrote again to say she'd like to try a session the following Saturday. She added, almost as an afterthought: *I will bring my boyfriend, yes? He wants to see, to make sure all okay.*

Roland stared at the screen, lips pressed tight. A boyfriend. That complicated things.

But it also provided cover. No one could accuse him of impropriety with a man sitting in the corner. He could not use the machine — of course not — but he could still play the part of the careful, attentive photographer.

When Saturday arrived, Roland was already at the stable, lamps set up, backdrop smooth. He heard the crunch of tyres on gravel and stepped outside just as the car pulled up.

Anna was Eastern European, younger than Emily, perhaps early-twenties, with long black hair and a striking sharpness to her cheekbones. Her accent was strong, her vowels round and heavy.

"This is nice," she said, glancing around the stable interior as she stepped inside. "Better than I thought. You make it look warm, like a real studio."

Her boyfriend followed — tall, broad-shouldered, eyes cautious but not hostile. He shook Roland's hand without a word, then folded himself into the chair at the side of the room, arms crossed.

The shoot began simply. Anna posed with a scarf, then in her jacket, smiling brightly at the camera. She needed little prompting; her confidence was natural, easy. Occasionally she looked toward her boyfriend, who gave a small nod, and she would laugh and shift into a new pose.

Roland worked carefully, his voice steady. He gave her gentle direction, flattering her with small compliments. "Turn your chin slightly — yes, perfect. That's elegant. Hold it there."

The boyfriend remained still, watchful.

No machine tonight. No secret hum in the background. Just the click of the shutter, the play of light on her face.

And yet, when Roland lowered the camera at last, Anna's smile was broad, genuine. "I like these," she said, peering at the preview on his screen. "You make me look…" She gestured, searching for the word. "…beautiful."

Her boyfriend gave a grudging smile, muttering something in his own tongue that made her laugh.

Before they left, Anna touched Roland's arm. "I tell my friend about this, yes? She would like. She is shy, but maybe I convince her."

Roland inclined his head, hiding the quickening of his pulse. "Of course. I'd be happy to meet her."

The car pulled away, leaving him in silence once more.

No machine. No arousal thick in the air.

But the door had opened again. Another woman. Another possibility.

And next time, perhaps, the boyfriend wouldn't be there.

Roland drove back to his bungalow as dusk settled, headlights carving through the hedgerows. The stable had been a clean success — no machine, no risk — but Anna's enthusiasm, her touch on his arm, lingered with him. And her parting words about her friend replayed over and over. *She is shy, but maybe I convince her.*

Back inside, he made tea and settled at his desk. The camera's memory card slid into the reader, and within seconds Anna's images filled the screen.

They were good. She had a natural presence, an openness to the lens that Emily had only discovered halfway through. A scarf draped over her shoulders, her smile wide and easy. Jacket off, hair spilling free, eyes alive with laughter.

Roland selected a neat batch — twelve frames, balanced and flattering — and began to prepare a proof set for her. He was halfway through the edits when a new notification flickered in the corner of the screen.

1 new message.

Emily.

He clicked it open, pulse quickening.

Roland,
I'd love to do another session. Thursday afternoon around 2pm
works best for me. I hope that suits you. I'm really looking
forward to it.

Roland sat back, the words burning on the screen.
Thursday. Two o'clock. She was coming back. And this
time, she would be his alone again — no boyfriend, no
watchful eyes. Just Emily, the camera, and the machine
waiting in the shadows.

He typed his reply carefully:

That works perfectly. I'll have everything prepared for you. It'll be
good to see you again.

He sent it, then turned back to Anna's folder. A few
more adjustments, a quick export, and he composed
another message:

Anna,
Thank you for today. It was a pleasure to meet with you both.
I've attached a selection of proofs for you to enjoy. Please let me
know if you'd like to arrange another session.

Attachments added. Message sent.

Roland leaned back, staring at the glow of the monitor.
Two women now tethered to him. Two threads pulling
tighter.

Anna — with her promise of a shy friend.

Emily — already returning, already hungry.

His cock stirred at the thought.

Thursday, he thought. Thursday would be the day he decided whether 14.6 was enough… or whether it was finally time for 3.3.

Chapter Twenty Five

Thursday.

Roland rose earlier than usual, the anticipation already stirring his cock. He moved through the stable with deliberate care, adjusting lamps, checking shadows, ensuring the backdrop was smooth. Every detail mattered now.

Emily was not coming as a curiosity this time. She was coming because she wanted it. And Roland intended to give her more than she had imagined.

He opened the large case he'd brought from the bungalow and laid its contents neatly on the table by the backdrop. Stockings, suspenders, sheer black bras, delicate lace knickers. A silk maid's outfit folded with precise care. Even a pair of long satin gloves, soft as water to the touch.

He paused, fingertips grazing the lingerie. Would she laugh? Blush? Or would the hum of 14.6 coax her into sliding one of these onto her body with a playful smile, her nipples hard beneath the lace?

The thought made him throb.

Roland placed a chair to the side, draping it with a shawl for her to pose against. He adjusted the camera tripod, tested the angles. The generator sat discreetly in the corner, its cables running to the twin towers on either side of the room. He gathered his thoughts, breathed in deeply and thought.

'The perfect beginning.'

He imagined Emily's arrival. Her smile as she stepped through the doorway, her nervous laugh. She would sit for the first few frames, clothed, teasing the lens with a tilt of her head, a careless grin. Then he would ease her, gently, into the hum. The laughter would loosen. Her blouse would unbutton again. Her confidence would bloom.

And when she was laughing topless, bra discarded, cheeks flushed, Roland would gesture toward the table. "Perhaps you'd like to try something different?"

She would glance at the lingerie, hesitate, then giggle as she lifted a pair of suspenders, holding them to her waist. And once she slipped them on, once the lace cupped her curves and the stockings slid up her thighs, she would look at him differently.

Her playful teasing would darken into hunger. And he — finally — would have the choice.

14.6 for daring.

Or 3.3 for surrender.

Roland stood in the silence of the stable, his cock straining against his trousers. He had never felt so alive, so powerful.

Emily would arrive in hours.

And by the end of the day, she would either leave with more photographs… or with his seed inside her.

At one fifty-seven, Roland checked the mirror in the small washroom for the third time. His shirt was buttoned, pressed; his hair combed back. He looked calm. Respectable. Professional.

Inside, his heart was hammering.

By the time the sound of tyres crunching on the gravel reached him, his cock was already stiff, pressing uncomfortably against his trousers. He forced himself to breathe slowly, straightening his collar before stepping outside.

Emily climbed out of her car with a small smile. She wore a light jacket over a pale blouse and slim jeans, her hair tied back loosely. Even dressed plainly, she had a glow about her — a quiet confidence that hadn't been there the first time.

"Hello again," she said warmly as she approached.

"Emily," Roland greeted, voice steady. "Good to see you again."

He held the stable door open, letting her step inside. She glanced around with an approving nod. "It looks even better than last time. You've really made it feel like a proper studio."

"Thank you. I've been refining things," Roland said, careful to keep his tone measured. He gestured toward the backdrop and the chair. "We'll start simply, as before. No rush."

Emily slipped off her jacket and laid it neatly over the chair. The blouse beneath clung gently to her frame; Roland's eyes lingered on the faint swell of her breasts before he forced himself to look away.

She smiled at him, as if catching the flicker of his gaze, then ran her hands down her jeans. "So, same as last time? Just posing, letting you direct me?"

"Yes," Roland replied quickly. He adjusted the camera, pretending to check the focus. "We'll take a few shots first. Keep it light, natural."

The generator sat silent in the corner, its towers waiting. He had not touched the dial yet. To do so would have been to betray himself, to risk her seeing the hunger in his eyes before the first photo was even taken.

No — he would wait. He would appear calm, respectful, professional.

Emily settled into the chair, crossing her legs casually, smiling toward the lens. "Ready when you are."

Roland lifted the camera, his hands only faintly trembling.

The machine was still silent. His cock was still straining.

But the game had only just begun.

The first few minutes were ordinary enough. Roland snapped shots of Emily leaning back in the chair, smiling lightly, brushing her hair from her face. She posed without fuss, but there was a restraint about her, a self-conscious edge, as if she was aware of every move.

He lowered the camera. "One moment. Let me just adjust something."

Crossing to the generator, he flicked the switch and eased the dial to **14.6**.

The hum filled the stable, soft and low, settling like a pulse beneath the floorboards.

Emily blinked, shifted in her seat, then gave a sudden, brighter smile. "Feels... different in here," she murmured, almost to herself.

"Different how?" Roland asked, raising the camera again.

She tilted her head, lips curling. "I don't know. Just... lighter. Like I don't have to think so much."

The shutter clicked.

Her posture changed — looser, more fluid. She lifted her arms, letting her blouse stretch across her chest, then laughed as though amused at her own boldness.

"Maybe I should try something... more fun," she said, sliding one leg over the arm of the chair. The denim pulled tight across her thighs, the seam pressing high between her legs, drawing Roland's eye to the clear outline of her sex.

His cock throbbed. He kept the camera steady.

"Yes," he said softly. "That's perfect."

Emily leaned forward now, elbows on her knees, chin resting in her palm. Her blouse gaped slightly, giving a glimpse of lace beneath. She held his gaze through the lens, a flicker of mischief in her eyes.

Another click.

She brushed her hair back, arching her spine deliberately, breasts pressing against the fabric. "Feels easier this time," she whispered. "Like I can just… let go."

Roland swallowed, cock straining painfully. "Then let go," he said.

Emily laughed — not nervously, but with a sultry edge. She slid a finger slowly down the front of her blouse, stopping just above the buttons. Her tongue darted across her lips as she looked into the lens.

Click. Click.

Roland could feel the ache rising in him, every muscle screaming to step forward, to touch her, to take. But he stayed rooted, camera in hand, letting the hum do its work.

Emily shifted again, this time reclining with her arms spread across the chair, one leg draped carelessly wide. "I feel like… teasing," she admitted, voice low. "Is that what you want me to do?"

Roland's breath caught. He steadied the camera, the words almost a growl. "Yes. Tease me."

And she did — running her hands down her thighs, arching her back, tilting her head with a playful, almost taunting smile.

The 14.6 was working. Loosening her, coaxing her deeper.

Roland's cock throbbed, but he held himself firm. Not yet.

Not until he decided.

Emily's fingers hovered at the buttons of her blouse, her smile widening. "Maybe I should go a little further," she whispered, almost as if daring herself.

Roland steadied the camera. "If you'd like to."

Her laugh was soft, breathy. She undid the first button, then the next, the blouse falling open to reveal the lace bra beneath. She slipped it from her shoulders, letting it hang loose before pushing it down her arms. The bra soon followed, unclasped with a practiced flick, tumbling to the chair beside her.

Her breasts rose proudly, nipples dark and stiff, the cool air teasing them into harder peaks. She cupped them playfully, lifting them, then dropped her hands with a grin, as though testing his control.

"Do you want this in the pictures?" she teased.

"Yes," Roland murmured, voice thick. The shutter clicked again and again.

Emily shifted in the chair, sliding forward so that her hips pressed to the edge. Her hands dropped to her waistband. She popped the button of her jeans and slowly tugged the zip down, the sound impossibly loud in the humming stable.

Roland's cock pulsed painfully.

She wriggled the denim over her hips, inch by inch, laughing at the awkwardness of the movement. "God, these are tight…" she muttered, pulling them down until they clung mid-thigh.

Beneath, her knickers clung close — black, netted, translucent. The dark mound of hair beneath was visible through the weave, the shadowed curls pressing against the thin fabric.

Emily leaned back, legs parted, one hand resting casually over her thigh as if offering herself to the lens. Her grin was wicked, daring. "Like this?"

Roland swallowed hard, his voice gravel. "Perfect. Don't move."

The shutter clicked again, capturing her breasts high and proud, her thighs spread, the outline of her sex framed by the netted fabric.

Emily giggled, rolling her hips slightly. "I feel… so naughty," she confessed, but her eyes glittered with excitement. "And I love it."

Roland could barely breathe. Every nerve in his body screamed to cross the space between them, to taste her, to bury himself in the heat he could almost see through the mesh.

But he stayed still, camera in hand, cock throbbing, letting the hum of 14.6 do the work.

Because this wasn't the moment to take.

This was the moment to watch.

The minutes stretched, thick with the low hum of the generator. Emily seemed to shed all trace of shyness. What began as a nervous unbuttoning had turned into a performance — and she relished every second.

She rose from the chair and walked barefoot across the rug, the denim of her jeans still clinging around her thighs, knickers sheer, her breasts swaying freely. She leaned forward against the wall, arching her back until her ass jutted out, round and firm. Turning her head, she cast Roland a wicked look over her shoulder.

"Like this?" she asked, voice playful, hips wiggling as if mocking his composure.

Roland clicked the shutter, his mouth dry. "Yes. Hold that."

She laughed, a breathless sound, and pressed her palms higher on the wall, stretching her spine so that her cheeks lifted, the mesh of her knickers tightening over her mound. The dark curls beneath were clearly visible now, teasing him with every shift of her hips.

Another click. Another.

Emily pushed back from the wall and sauntered toward the chair again, her grin daring. She sat on its edge, legs parted, lifting her breasts in her hands and pressing them up until her tongue flicked over her own nipples. A low giggle escaped her throat as if the taste surprised her.

Roland groaned under his breath, his cock throbbing hard enough to ache.

She squeezed them together, thrusting them forward, eyes half-lidded as she teased the camera. "You're really going to send me these, aren't you?" she whispered.

"Yes," Roland managed. His hand shook on the camera, but the shutter never stopped.

Emily shifted again, dropping to her knees on the rug. She leaned forward, resting on her elbows, arching her back so that her ass lifted high. Looking back over her shoulder, hair falling across her cheek, she gave a mischievous bite of her lip.

The jeans slid lower with her movements, caught now around her knees. She spread them wider, the mesh knickers stretched taut across her ass, the shape of her slit pressed clearly against the fabric.

Roland's breath came ragged. Every click of the shutter was torture and ecstasy at once.

For fifteen minutes, Emily flowed from pose to pose — straddling the chair backwards, bending low with her breasts swinging, crawling across the rug like a cat. Each gesture bolder than the last, her laughter spilling freely, her arousal written in the flush of her skin and the stiffness of her nipples.

It was as though the hum of 14.6 had stripped away every restraint, leaving only mischief, daring, and the hunger to show herself.

Roland knew he could end it at any moment. He could flick the dial higher, to 3.3, and she would be his entirely.

But he didn't.

He stayed behind the lens, cock straining, savouring the knowledge that he could.

That was enough.

Roland lowered the camera at last, his chest rising and falling as though he'd been running. Emily knelt on the rug before him, hair wild, breasts flushed, the mesh of her knickers stretched taut over her cunt.

She tilted her head, grinning. "Is that all you brought for me to play with?"

Roland hesitated, then stepped to the table at the side of the room. He unclipped the latches of a black case and lifted the lid. Inside, neatly arranged, lay the pieces he had chosen days ago — silk stockings, suspender belts, lace bras, a satin maid's outfit folded in perfect lines.

Emily rose, padding toward him, eyes shining with curiosity. She trailed her fingers over the items, humming softly as if choosing sweets from a jar.

"Well," she murmured, glancing up at him, "aren't you prepared."

Roland swallowed. "They're just… options. Props, if you wanted to—"

She cut him off with a laugh, tugging the suspenders free and holding them to her waist. "Props? Oh no. These are temptations."

Her voice lowered, a sultry edge creeping in. "Tell me… what do 'you' like, Roland?"

He felt his throat tighten. His cock ached inside his trousers, but he forced the words out. "Stockings. Suspenders. And the maid's outfit."

Emily's smile widened. She set the suspenders down and lifted the folded satin from the case. "The maid's outfit, hmm? Naughty man." She unfolded it slowly, letting the glossy fabric spill over her arms. "You like the idea of me serving you?"

Her laughter was playful, but her eyes gleamed with challenge. She pressed the outfit to her chest, nipples peeking above the neckline as if testing the size. Then she glanced back at him, lips curling.

"Hold-up stockings too, you said?"

Roland nodded stiffly, his cock throbbing. "Yes."

Emily pulled a pair free from the case, running the sheer fabric over her cheek before draping it over her shoulder. "Mmm. I think I like that idea too."

She stepped back, holding the maid's dress in one hand, the stockings in the other. "Shall I?" she asked, her grin wicked.

Roland's breath came slow, heavy. His hand twitched over the dial of the generator, but he didn't move it. Not yet.

"Yes," he said hoarsely. "Put them on."

Emily giggled and slipped behind the dressing screen at the corner of the stable, her silhouette a blur through the frosted wood. The sound of fabric rustled, jeans sliding down, knickers tugged away, satin whispering as it slid over her skin.

Roland stood frozen, cock aching, every nerve lit.

When Emily stepped out again, the maid's outfit hugged her curves, short enough to flash the tops of her thighs. The hold-up stockings gleamed against her skin, the black lace band biting into the softness above her knees.

She placed her hands on her hips, breasts pressing against the satin, and gave him a cheeky curtsey.

"Ready for service, sir."

Roland nearly groaned aloud.

The machine's hum filled the silence, steady at **14.6**.

Emily was his playful maid now — and he had not even touched the 3.3.

Emily moved with a new kind of grace in the outfit, each gesture exaggerated, sultry, almost mocking. She bent at the waist, polishing an invisible surface with her palm, her ass raised high, the hem of the satin dress sliding up to reveal the lace tops of her stockings.

Roland snapped photos, his hand trembling.

She spun, pressed her back to the wall, and tugged the neckline lower until her breasts spilled free once more. She cupped them, pinched her nipples, and stuck her tongue out playfully, running it across her lips as though presenting herself to be tasted.

"Do you like your maid like this?" she teased, voice low, sultry.

Roland's cock pulsed painfully. Every muscle screamed. He lowered the camera, his eyes locked on her flushed skin, her hunger growing with every pose.

His hand drifted to the dial. For weeks he had restrained himself, keeping her balanced at the playful edge of 14.6. But now, watching her grinding her hips against the chair, breasts bare, stockings gleaming — he couldn't hold back any longer.

Slowly, he twisted the dial down. **3.3.**

The hum changed, deepened, vibrating through the very air.

Emily froze mid-pose, her lips parting. A shudder ran through her, from the swell of her breasts down to her stockinged thighs. She gasped sharply, then moaned, her hand flying between her legs, gripping herself through the satin.

"Oh… oh god… Roland…"

Her eyes glazed with heat. She staggered forward a step, clutching his arm, her breasts pressed against his sleeve.

The maid's dress clung to her sweat-damp skin as she writhed.

"Please," she whispered, almost desperate. "I can't... I can't stop it. I need—" Her words broke into a moan as her hips bucked.

Roland's cock throbbed, his control hanging by a thread. He had seen the shift before in theory — Sam, the parties — but never like this, never directed solely at him.

Emily wasn't posing anymore. She was pleading.

Her knickers were already damp, the lace of her stockings glistening where her thighs rubbed. She clutched his shirt, pulling him closer, eyes wild. "Roland... I need cock. Please. Yours."

The maid was gone.

The playful tease was gone.

In her place was raw, unrelenting lust — unleashed by 3.3.

Roland's breath caught in his throat as her hand fumbled at his belt, tugging frantically. He looked down at her, her breasts heaving, her lips swollen, her thighs trembling with need.

He had imagined this moment countless times.

Now it was here.

And Emily wanted nothing but to be fucked.

Emily's fingers clawed at his belt, tugging with frantic urgency. The buckle clinked open, and she yanked at his zip, her breath hot, her eyes wild with hunger.

"Emily—wait—you don't know what you're—" Roland began, but his voice cracked, his cock already throbbing against the fabric.

"I do know," she cut him off, almost snarling the words. "I want it. I need it. Please—your cock—I need it in my mouth, now."

Her hand plunged into his trousers, wrapping around his thick, swollen length. She moaned at the feel of him, pumping him roughly as she dropped to her knees, satin brushing the floor, stockings tight over her thighs.

Roland's head tipped back, a guttural groan escaping his throat as her lips pressed to the tip, wet and hot. She took him into her mouth with desperate greed, sucking hard, moaning as if she were starving.

Her free hand dove between her thighs, tugging her knickers aside. He glimpsed the dark hair beneath, glistening wet, her fingers plunging into her wet cunt as she devoured him.

"Christ—Emily—" Roland gasped, his hands sinking into her hair, guiding her rhythm.

She bobbed faster, saliva slicking his cock, her eyes up on him, wide and glazed with lust. Her muffled moans vibrated down his shaft as she fingered herself furiously, hips rocking against her own hand.

The hum of **3.3** pulsed through the air, through their bodies, amplifying every movement, every sound. It wasn't just sex — it was raw compulsion, primal need, their bodies tuned to the same desperate frequency.

Emily gagged as he pushed deeper, then moaned around his cock, drool spilling down her chin. She pulled back with a gasp, eyes wild.

"Fuck me, Roland—please—I need you inside me—" she begged, grinding her soaked fingers harder into her cunt. "I'll do anything—just fuck me—"

Roland's restraint shattered. He yanked her to her feet, spun her against the chair, the maid's dress riding high over her hips. Her stockings gleamed as he shoved her knickers aside, his cock pressed to her dripping slit.

Emily screamed as he thrust into her, her body arching, breasts bouncing as she clutched the chair.

The frenzy consumed them. Her cries, his grunts, the slap of flesh on flesh echoing through the stable. She fucked him back with equal hunger, meeting every thrust, her cunt gripping him, milking him, begging him to spill inside.

"Harder—oh god, harder—" she cried, clawing at the wood as her orgasm built, her body convulsing in waves.

Roland roared, driving deep, and came with her, filling her, pumping thick ropes into her spasming cunt.

They collapsed together, slick with sweat, the machine still humming low in the corner as though indifferent to the chaos it had wrought.

Emily's voice was hoarse, breathless, trembling against his ear.

"I've never... never felt anything like that," she whispered, shuddering. "Don't ever... stop."

Roland clutched her tighter, cock still throbbing inside her.

He didn't plan to.

Not now.

Not ever.

Roland meant to pull out, meant to regain some measure of control — but Emily wouldn't let him. Her legs locked around his hips, her nails dug into his back, her cries rising higher with every brutal thrust.

"Don't stop—don't you dare stop!" she screamed, her body convulsing around him, another orgasm ripping through her.

Roland groaned, hips pounding, her cunt milking him with every clench. He'd already emptied once, thick and hot inside her, but his cock stayed hard, throbbing as if untouched. The **3.3** hum coursed through him like a drug, demanding more.

He grabbed her waist, spun her onto her hands and knees. Her ass lifted high, stockings biting into her thighs, the maid's skirt bunched around her hips. He drove into her from behind, his balls slapping wetly against her, her screams echoing off the walls.

"Fuck! Yes—fuck me harder!" Emily shrieked, hair flying, saliva spilling from her open mouth. She reached between her thighs, rubbing herself furiously as his cock pistoned in and out, the sound wet and savage.

Roland felt himself cresting again, groaning deep. He pulled free at the last second, jerking his cock over her arched back. Hot, thick jets of cum sprayed across her shoulder blades, glistening on her flushed skin.

Emily moaned at the sensation, spinning onto her back before he'd even caught his breath. She gripped his cock with both hands, pumping it, smearing his cum over his shaft and her breasts.

"Again—please, in my mouth—" she begged, eyes blazing with desperation.

Roland staggered forward, and she swallowed him greedily, sucking him deep, her throat convulsing as she took every inch. He groaned, hips jerking, his seed spilling once more into her hungry mouth. She gulped it down, licking her lips, begging for more even as it dribbled down her chin.

But still his cock stayed hard.

The **3.3 wouldn't release him**.

Emily dropped to all fours, her ass swaying, eyes glazed with need. "Again. Please. I can't stop. Fuck me again!"

And he did. On the rug, against the wall, straddled across the chair. Her cries filled the stable, her orgasms tearing through her one after another, until she was shaking, trembling, her body slick with sweat and cum.

Roland's own releases came like waves, hot and endless — inside her, across her tits, splattering her face, pumping into her mouth. Every time he thought he was spent, the machine drove him on, his cock iron-hard, his body refusing to rest.

It was relentless.

They were trapped in it, devouring each other, clawing, sucking, thrusting, until neither knew where one ended and the other began.

Only when Roland's trembling hand finally twisted the dial, snapping it back to zero, did the hum die.

Silence crashed into the room like a flood.

Emily collapsed onto the rug, body limp, her chest heaving, face and breasts streaked with his cum. Her eyes fluttered open slowly, dazed but glowing.

Roland fell beside her, his cock still wet, still half-hard, but at last softening as the last tremors of the frequency faded.

Emily smiled faintly, her lips swollen, her voice hoarse.

"Roland... that was... fucking insane."

She laughed weakly, licking her lips. "I've never... I've never come so much in my life."

Roland lay back, staring at the ceiling, his own body wrecked, his cock aching.

The truth settled cold and electric in his chest.

With **3.3**, there was no limit.

No stopping.

No escape.

They lay tangled on the rug, their bodies slick and spent, the stable thick with the scent of sex. The machine was silent again, but only Roland knew why — to Emily it had been nothing more than passion, raw and impossible to resist.

Emily shifted onto her back, breathing hard, her nipples still tight, her thighs trembling with aftershocks. Yet she was smiling, her face glowing in the low light.

"Roland…" she whispered, almost laughing. "I don't know what you did to me… but it was unreal. I've never felt anything like that. Ever."

She rolled toward him, brushing her fingers over his chest. "We have to do it again. Promise me."

Roland swallowed, his heart still hammering. "It was… intense," he said carefully.

"Intense?" She laughed breathlessly, kissing his shoulder. "That was more than intense. That was… unstoppable. You made me feel like I couldn't stop, like I didn't want to stop."

Her hand drifted to his cock, giving it a playful squeeze. "And you just kept going… god, Roland. Do you realise what you did to me?"

He said nothing, only stroked her hair back, watching her eyes burn with a mixture of wonder and hunger.

"Next time," she whispered, her voice sultry, "maybe we should film it. Us together. So I can watch it back when I'm alone…" She bit her lip, her cheeks flushed, her eyes full of mischief.

She stood slowly, pulling on her jeans with shaky fingers, her breasts still bare until she finally slipped her blouse back over them. At the door she paused, glancing at his camera.

"Send me all the photos. Every single one. I want to keep them." Her smile turned sly. "They'll remind me. And… they'll keep me thinking about when I can come back."

Roland nodded, his throat dry.

She lowered her voice to a whisper. "Nobody can know about this. Not with the age difference. People wouldn't understand." She smiled again, almost girlish this time. "But I don't care. I just want more of you."

Then she was gone, leaving Roland alone in the quiet stable.

Only he knew the truth.

It hadn't been him alone.

It had been the machine.

And with it, he could have this again. With Emily. With anyone.

✦ ✦ ✦

Chapter Twenty Six

Back at the bungalow that evening, Roland transferred the files from his camera to the laptop. The screen filled with image after image of Emily — playful, daring, half-dressed, then topless, then spread wide in her stockings and maid's outfit.

For a moment he hovered, considering which ones to send. He could curate them, give her only the lighter poses, keep the rawest, filthiest frames for himself.

But then he remembered her words, her insistence. *All of them.*

With a slow exhale, he attached the entire set to his reply.

Here are your photographs. All unedited, as promised. They are yours.
– Roland

His finger tapped **Send,** and the deed was done. The images were hers now — reminders of what she'd felt, proof of what they'd shared. Proof that she would crave it again.

He sat back in the chair, his cock twitching as he thought of her suggestion: filming next time. The idea refused to leave his mind. Emily, on her knees, looking up into the camera with his cock between her lips — it made him ache all over again.

The computer chimed. A new message.

Roland opened it, expecting perhaps Emily's reply, but the name was different. Anna.

He scanned the text, his pulse quickening.

Anna thanked him again for her photographs, telling him how confident and beautiful she had felt. But this time she added something more: she had shown the pictures to a friend. A close friend who had been impressed. Excited. Curious.

And now both of them wanted a photo session.

No mention of the boyfriend this time. No interference. Just Anna… and another young woman, ready to step into his stable.

Roland sat in silence, staring at the words.

His mind raced with images — two women laughing together in front of his lens, loosening under the hum, daring each other, touching, kissing, spreading wide while he decided if — and when — to shift the dial to 3.3.

His cock stirred again, stiffening against his trousers. Emily already wanted him back, begging for secrecy, hungry for more. And now Anna was bringing reinforcements.

The machine had opened the door.

And women were walking through it.

Chapter Twenty Seven

Roland wasn't expecting visitors. The last week had been a blur of images — Emily in stockings, Emily arching her back, Emily's eyes wet with lust — and now Anna's next email was waiting for his reply. He was halfway through typing when the knock at his door startled him.

Through the curtain, he saw Sam.

She stood in her garden jacket, hands tucked in her pockets, hair tied back in that easy, practical knot he'd seen a hundred times before. A neighbour. A friend. A reminder of the days when this machine had been nothing more than an experiment for sore joints.

Roland opened the door with his best smile, though his stomach tightened.

"Alright, Sam," he said, leaning on the frame as though casual.

"Got a minute?" she asked.

"Of course."

She stepped inside, bringing a gust of cool afternoon air with her. She didn't sit, not yet — just glanced around his bungalow like she was searching for something.

"What can I do for you?" he asked, careful to sound casual.

Sam leaned against the counter, arms folded. "It's that machine of yours. The scalar thing. The one you said you'd sold."

Roland nodded slowly. "Yes. That's right. Sold it off."

"I know." She waved a hand, dismissing that detail. "But here's the thing. I've got a friend. She's been struggling with chronic pain — hips, back, the works. Pills don't touch it. I told her about what you'd been fiddling with before you sold it on. And now she wants one. She asked me straight out if I could find where to buy it."

Roland kept his face still, though his pulse quickened.

"And?"

"So I thought I'd ask you." She leaned closer, eyes sharp. "Where did you get it from?"

For a heartbeat too long, Roland said nothing. The real answer — the late-night order, the obscure website, the technical forums that had fed his obsession — sat like fire on his tongue. If Sam had the name, the link, the model number, she'd dig. She'd find it. And then the secret of 3.3 would be out of his hands.

"I honestly can't remember," he said finally, shrugging. "It was one of those niche suppliers online. Not Amazon. One of those health gadget sites that pop up in adverts."

Sam frowned. "You must have some record. A receipt? An email?"

Roland shook his head. "Old laptop died last month, wiped half my inbox with it. If I had the details, I'd pass them on. But it's gone. Sorry."

She studied him for a long moment, her lips pursed. She didn't quite believe him — he could see that — but she didn't push further.

"Well," she said eventually, "that's a shame. My friend would've paid good money. She's desperate."

Roland softened his tone. "Tell her to look into bio-resonance therapy. Or PEMF machines. There are alternatives. She might find something that helps."

Sam nodded reluctantly, then gave him a small smile. "I thought it was worth asking. You were always tinkering with that thing, I thought you'd know."

"Sorry, Sam," Roland said again, watching as she headed back out into the garden.

He closed the door slowly and leaned against it, exhaling.

She was circling too close. The machine, the field, the truth of what he was doing in the stable — it all needed to remain buried.

Sam couldn't know. No one could.

✦ ✦ ✦

Chapter Twenty Eight

The rest of the day, Roland couldn't shake Sam's face from his mind — that sharp, questioning look when she asked where he'd bought the machine. She wasn't convinced by his story, he could feel it. She'd left with a smile, but it wasn't finished, not really.

He told himself it didn't matter. The machine was hidden, the stable was secure, and Sam had no way of tracing it. Still, it itched at him. A neighbour too curious could undo everything.

So, he buried himself back in what mattered: the shoots.

That night, Roland sat at his desk, fingers hovering over the keyboard. Anna's last email was open, still unread since morning. Her words were simple, almost innocent:

Roland returned to the email he had started to send to Anna.

then began to type.

Dear Anna,

Thank you for your message. I would be happy to arrange a shoot for you and your friend. Please let me know which days are best for you, and I will confirm availability. I would recommend an afternoon session for the best natural light in the studio.

As with all my shoots, please note I ask that no alcohol or recreational drugs are taken before the session — it interferes with the energy of the photos and affects the results.

I look forward to hearing from you.

Best wishes,
Roland

He read it over carefully before clicking **Send**.

Then, for a moment, he sat back and let himself imagine it: two women instead of one. The stable filled with laughter, nervous at first, then loosening, relaxing. The familiar hum of 14.6 in the air. Playfulness turning to daring. The gradual slide from innocence to heat.

And if he wished, just a flick of the dial down to 3.3.

Roland swallowed, shifting uncomfortably in his chair as his cock hardened at the thought. He was in control. Every choice, every second, belonged to him.

A notification pinged. Another email.

This time from Emily.

She was brief, but her words tightened every nerve in his body:

"Roland, I can't stop thinking about our last session. When can we do it again?"

He stared at the screen, pulse hammering, two opportunities staring him in the face — Emily, already proven, already his. And Anna, bringing fresh temptation with a friend.

Roland smiled slowly.

The machine had been purchased to heal. Now it was practised for lust. And the hunger for it was spreading.

Roland stayed at the desk long after the emails were sent, the glow of the monitor casting thin shadows across his bungalow walls. He wasn't working now — he was plotting.

Emily. Anna. A friend he didn't yet know.

Three names. Two more possibilities.

He rubbed at his chin, recalling the heat in Emily's voice when she'd begged for more. She hadn't been shy about what she wanted. 'Film us together next time.' Her words echoed in his head, teasing, daring.

Filming. That was no small decision. Photographs were easy enough to manage, edit, send. But video? That would bind her to him in a different way. It would be proof. Not just of her body, but of her submission — the way the machine bent her into lust. If she ever doubted what they had done, all he'd need to do was replay the footage.

Still, it wasn't without risk. Files could be traced. Shared. Lost. He would need an external drive, something secure, hidden away from the prying eyes of neighbours. From Sam.

He made a note of it in his small leather notebook: *Camera tripod. External hard drive. Lockbox.*

Then his thoughts shifted back to Anna. She had been sweet enough. He wasn't sure what to expect with her friend, but Eastern European women had a certain bluntness he found refreshing. They said what they wanted, they didn't circle around it. That could work in his favour.

But two women at once... the dynamic would be different. He'd need to manage it carefully. If one grew shy while the other became bold, the balance might tip. He couldn't risk panic. Not yet. Not until he knew how strong their resistance was.

14.6 would be the key. Just enough to spark playfulness, to loosen them into laughter and daring. Not the full plunge of 3.3 — not unless they begged for it.

Roland smiled, already picturing the stable lit with candles, the soft hum in the air, his camera ready.

Emily would be his indulgence — the filmed session, the private record. Anna and her friend would be the experiment, his test of how the field handled more than one at a time.

It was coming together now, each piece sliding neatly into place.

Roland closed the laptop at last, leaning back in his chair. The faint pulse of arousal lingered in his body, the same steady beat he always felt when the plan crystallised in his mind.

He had control. Over Emily, over Anna, over what came next.

And no one — not Sam, not her curious friend, not a soul in this town — had any idea.

✦ ✦ ✦

Chapter Twenty Nine

Roland read Emily's email again, her words still glowing on the screen.

"Roland, I can't stop thinking about our last session. When can we do it again?"

His cock twitched at the memory — her kneeling, pleading, eyes glazed with lust as she begged for more. She had been transformed, and now she wanted to return willingly. He had her exactly where he wanted.

But he also remembered her request. *Film us together next time.*

Roland tapped the desk with his fingertips. He couldn't afford to fumble this. If he brushed off the filming, she might drift away, assume he wasn't serious, or worse — find someone else. Yet if he rushed into it unprepared, he risked sloppy evidence.

He opened a reply and began typing, each word chosen with precision.

Dear Emily,

It makes me smile to know you enjoyed our last session so much. I would be very happy to arrange another. You mentioned wanting to capture it on film, and I agree — but I want to do it properly. A good camera, lighting, sound — the works. Something you'll be proud to keep.

I'll need a little time to set it up right. Consider it part of the anticipation. Once everything is in place, we can meet again and make sure we capture every moment exactly as you imagined.

In the meantime, I want to be sure you're still keen. Filming is a different kind of intimacy. If you're certain, then I'll go ahead and prepare.

Best,
Roland

He sat back, reading it over twice before hitting **Send**.

Polite. Professional. Respectful. But beneath it, the message was clear: he wasn't letting her slip away.

He could already imagine her reply. Eager. Hungry. Maybe impatient. That impatience was good — it would keep her coming back.

Roland leaned back in his chair, smiling faintly. Emily's film would be his private archive, a record of the machine's true power. Every glance, every moan, every thrust — captured forever.

He'd need to order a tripod. A better lens. Perhaps even a wireless mic, to catch the breathless edge in her voice. He scribbled another note in his book.

Yes. When Emily returned, it would be perfect.

But in the meantime, Anna and her friend were waiting. And with them, another kind of experiment entirely.

Roland closed his notebook just as another notification chimed. Another email.

Anna.

He clicked it open.

"Hello Roland, my friend and I are free this Saturday afternoon. Around three o'clock, if that works for you. We are both very excited to try. Thank you."

Roland felt his lips curl into a slow smile.

Saturday. Just a few days away. That gave him enough time to ready the stable again, polish the camera lenses, and prepare the case of outfits — stockings, lace, silk — all neatly folded, all waiting for eager hands.

He drafted his reply quickly, fingers steady:

Dear Anna,

Saturday at three will be perfect. I'll make sure the studio is prepared. As mentioned before, please avoid alcohol or recreational drugs before the shoot — it will help you both feel at ease and get the best results.

I look forward to meeting you both.

Best wishes,
Roland

When he clicked **Send**, his heart was already racing. Emily was safely tethered, her hunger kept alive while he set the stage for something new. And now Anna was returning — with a friend in tow.

The image filled his mind as he prepared that evening: the stable lit softly, the two women stepping nervously inside, their laughter bouncing off the stone walls, their accents colouring every word. He would greet them as a gentleman, calm and reassuring. He would guide them into poses, start with simple portraits — and then, when the moment was right, let the hum of 14.6 fill the air.

Roland could already see them loosening, growing playful. He could imagine the way their glances would shift from shy to daring. And if their resistance dissolved in sync…

He swallowed, hard.

The machine was patient. And so was he.

Saturday couldn't come soon enough.

✦ ✦ ✦

Chapter Thirty

Saturday arrived with a low grey sky, the kind of weather that suited Roland perfectly. It meant no one would be strolling out this way, no curious walkers glancing toward the old stable. The track was quiet, the field damp with last night's rain.

Roland had been there since morning, preparing. Fresh sheets hung against the back wall to serve as a backdrop. His lights were tested and set at flattering angles. The camera was mounted, its memory card cleared. Even the small electric heater hummed gently in the corner, warming the stone floor so the women wouldn't feel a chill.

At two fifty-eight, he heard the crunch of tyres on gravel.

A dark hatchback pulled up, and Anna stepped out first. She wore a simple black coat and smiled shyly when she saw him waiting at the door. Behind her came a taller woman with long blonde hair, striking in her features, her accent noticeable even before she spoke.

"Roland?" the blonde asked, offering her hand with a faint smile. "I'm Irena."

Her grip was firm, her eyes curious.

"Lovely to meet you," Roland said warmly, shaking it. "Come in, both of you. Out of the cold."

Inside, the stable looked more like a modest studio than a barn. The women glanced around, visibly relieved at its clean, professional setup. That was important — he had made sure of it.

"So," Roland said, gesturing to the camera. "How would you like to begin? Together, or separately?"

Anna and Irena exchanged a glance, then both laughed lightly.

"Together," Anna said. "We are friends, so… together is fine."

"Perfect," Roland replied, his chest tightening with anticipation. Together meant less hesitation. It meant shared laughter, shared daring — exactly what 14.6 would magnify.

For now, though, he kept everything professional. He showed them the rack of outfits — simple dresses, scarves, blouses, skirts. Neutral tones. Safe choices to start. They agreed on matching white blouses and dark jeans, a balance of casual and coordinated.

The first few shots were stiff, as he expected. Anna's smile was nervous, Irena's posture almost too rigid. But Roland spoke softly, guiding them into small movements, letting them lean into one another, laugh at the awkwardness, turn their shoulders slightly, tilt their chins just so.

Click. Click. Click.

On the viewfinder, they already looked beautiful. But Roland's mind was on the dial hidden at the back of the table. The generator waited, the two towers standing like silent sentries at opposite ends of the stable.

When the time was right, when the laughter flowed easily enough, he would let the field hum into life.

For now, he smiled behind the camera, his tone smooth and encouraging.

"That's it. Perfect. You two are naturals. Just relax into it — pretend I'm not even here."

They laughed again, leaning closer, Anna's arm around Irena's waist. The ice was melting. The session had begun.

And Roland's finger twitched, itching for the switch.

It didn't take long for the stiffness to ease. Anna and Irena began to move more freely, smiling at each other rather than at the camera. Anna leaned into her friend's shoulder, Irena flicked her blonde hair back with a laugh, their bodies naturally drifting closer as if some invisible tether pulled them inward.

Roland kept the camera raised, clicking steadily, his voice calm and encouraging. But his other hand reached down, fingers brushing the dial.

A soft hum filled the stable. Barely audible — more felt than heard.

14.6.

The field spread out, invisible, enveloping the three of them in its quiet charge. Roland stayed behind the camera, but he didn't need to move. The effect was immediate.

Anna's laughter deepened, looser, more unguarded. She tilted her head back, her blouse gaping slightly at the collar as she leaned into Irena's arm. Irena's eyes sparkled, her lips curling into a more daring smile as she rested her hand on Anna's hip — casual, but not entirely innocent.

Click. Click. Click.

Roland's cock stirred as he watched through the lens. The machine was doing its work. Every pose grew bolder, every gesture more playful. Anna puckered her lips at the camera, then at Irena. Irena, grinning, nudged her nose against Anna's cheek, their laughter bubbling like champagne.

"Perfect," Roland murmured. "Just keep moving together, natural, like that."

The women swayed, their arms winding more easily around each other's waists now. Their smiles softened into something warmer, their bodies pressing together in ways that went beyond simple posing.

Click. Click.

Anna's hand slipped lower on Irena's back, her fingers brushing the top of her friend's jeans. Irena didn't pull away. Instead, she giggled and leaned even closer, her cheek brushing Anna's.

Roland swallowed, adjusting his stance behind the camera. The air in the stable felt heavier, charged with the same pulse that was already tightening in his trousers.

Through the lens, he watched them change. Two friends, once stiff and polite, now playful, daring, and just beginning to slide into something more.

And the machine hummed on.

The laughter grew louder, looser, and their movements bolder. Anna gave Irena a cheeky grin and pressed her palm lightly against her friend's breast, almost as if to see what she'd do.

Irena squealed and swatted her hand away — but only to retaliate. Her own hand cupped Anna's breast, squeezing more deliberately. Both of them burst into giggles, their cheeks flushed, their bodies writhing against each other.

Click. Click.

Roland adjusted the lens, his cock stiff and straining against his trousers.

Irena gave Anna a playful smack on her backside, the sound echoing in the stable. Anna yelped, laughed, then returned the favour with a slap of her own. The giggling turned infectious, their energy filling the room, bouncing off the stone walls.

The hum of 14.6 deepened their play, loosening them, pulling away the natural hesitations of friends. Their hands lingered longer, their touches slid lower, until finally Anna brushed her lips against Irena's cheek.

Not staged. Not posed.

Real.

Irena turned her face, and their mouths met. The first kiss was brief, testing, but then they fell into it — deeper, hungrier, still laughing between breaths.

Roland's finger worked the shutter in rapid bursts. Click, click, click — capturing each moment as they pressed together, their breasts flattening against each other, hands roaming as though permission was no longer needed.

When at last they broke apart, Anna was breathless, her eyes wild with a mix of mischief and heat. She looked straight at Roland, lips swollen from kissing.

"Can we… go topless?" she asked, her voice low but certain.

Irena, still flushed and smiling, nodded eagerly beside her. "Yes. Together."

Roland lowered the camera slightly, his pulse hammering in his ears.

Professional. Calm. Always calm.

"If that's what you want," he said smoothly.

But inside, every nerve burned with anticipation.

The machine hummed on, and the stable grew hotter.

Anna didn't wait for further reassurance. Her fingers went to the buttons of her blouse, popping them one by one with deliberate slowness, her eyes never leaving Roland's lens. Irena mirrored her, tugging at the hem of her own blouse until both women shrugged them from their shoulders and let them fall to the stable floor.

Their bras followed in quick succession, lacy straps sliding down smooth arms until their breasts spilled free.

Roland swallowed hard behind the camera, his cock pressing painfully against his trousers.

Anna gave a cheeky grin and cupped her own breasts, squeezing them together before leaning into Irena. The blonde laughed, then reached across to pinch one of Anna's nipples, twisting it lightly until Anna squealed.

"Your turn," Anna teased, and without hesitation, she pinched Irena back. Both dissolved into giggles, their cheeks flushed, their bare breasts brushing against one another.

Click. Click.

Roland captured every second — the flushed skin, the playful touches, the way their movements grew more daring with each passing moment.

Then Anna leaned down, lips brushing across Irena's chest, before closing around her nipple. She sucked gently, flicking her tongue while Irena gasped, her laughter melting into a breathless moan.

Irena's hand tangled in Anna's hair, holding her close, before she pushed her back and returned the gesture — sucking Anna's nipple with equal playfulness, her teeth grazing just enough to make her friend gasp.

Roland's heart pounded as he clicked away, the air in the stable heavy, electric, charged. The hum of the generator seemed louder now, resonating in every movement, every laugh, every gasp of pleasure.

Two women, topless, breasts pressed together, nipples pinched and teased, mouths sucking and laughing all at once.

And Roland, hidden behind the lens, capturing it all while his cock ached for release.

The machine was working exactly as intended.

Their giggles bounced off the stone walls, louder now, freer, the kind of laughter that came with wine, or secrets — only this time it was the hum of 14.6 winding through them, loosening every barrier.

Anna tugged lightly at Irena's nipple with her teeth, then pulled back, saying something in quick, lilting words Roland couldn't catch. The sound of it made Irena burst into laughter, her cheeks pink, her eyes bright.

She replied in their own tongue, her voice husky, before both women collapsed into giggles again — clutching each other's breasts as though they needed the contact to stay upright.

Roland adjusted the camera, pretending to focus through the viewfinder. But then he noticed it — their eyes flicking toward him, not at his face, not at the lens, but lower.

Down at his crotch.

The bulge in his trousers was impossible to hide now. His cock strained hard against the fabric, the ache deep and pulsing.

Anna smirked, whispered something into Irena's ear in that same flowing language. Irena's hand shot up to cover her mouth as she laughed, her gaze darting back down at Roland's lap.

Click. Click.

He kept shooting, but his palms were damp, his pulse hammering in his ears. They were talking about him. About his cock. About the erection pressing against his trousers while he played the role of calm, professional photographer.

Anna tilted her head, grinning mischievously as she sucked her own nipple for show, her eyes still flicking to Roland. Irena giggled, slapped her ass lightly, then whispered something else that made them both howl with laughter.

The teasing was obvious now. Not cruel, but conspiratorial — a game between them, with him as the unspoken target.

Roland's mouth was dry. His finger hovered over the shutter, clicking automatically, capturing everything while his cock throbbed harder with every stolen glance.

The machine hummed, steady, relentless, feeding their playfulness, feeding his arousal.

And Roland knew he was balancing on a knife's edge.

The laughter slowed, softening into sly little giggles as both women looked at each other, then back at Roland. Anna tilted her head, eyes narrowing playfully as her hand slid down her own stomach, just above the waistband of her jeans.

"You... very hard," she said in her thick accent, her gaze fixed brazenly on the bulge in his trousers.

Irena smirked, covering her mouth as if to hide her grin, but her eyes betrayed her. They too flicked down, lingering there.

Roland froze behind the camera, his mouth dry.

"I—" he began, but Anna cut him off with a mischievous laugh.

"Don't be shy," she teased, her voice lilting, deliberately accented. "We can see."

Irena giggled again, whispering something in her own language. Anna burst out laughing, then translated between fits of giggles: "She says… maybe it is too big for trousers."

They collapsed into laughter together, their bare breasts shaking as they clung to each other, their eyes still locked on his bulge.

Click. Click. His hand trembled slightly on the shutter.

Anna's expression sobered just enough to add, more directly: "We want to see. You show us?"

Her smile was daring now, the kind of smile that knew the power of the request. Irena echoed it, nodding slowly, biting her lip as her eyes once more travelled down to his crotch.

The machine hummed. The air thickened. The two topless women leaned together, their nipples brushing as they waited, laughing softly, daring him.

Roland's cock throbbed against the fabric, aching with the weight of their gaze.

The choice was his.

Roland steadied his breath. The dial still sat at 14.6, humming low, steady. It was enough. He didn't need to push further. Not yet.

Anna and Irena had already crossed the line on their own — laughter turned daring, daring turned into hunger. Their eyes fixed on the bulge straining against his trousers, and their giggles softened into something else entirely.

"Show us," Anna murmured again, her accent heavy, her grin playful but certain.

Roland lowered the camera slowly, setting it aside. His heart pounded, but his face remained calm, measured, professional.

"You really want to see?" he asked, voice low.

Both women nodded in unison, their hair brushing together as they leaned forward.

Anna was the first to move. She stepped closer, fingers slipping to his belt buckle. Irena followed, crouching down beside her, eyes wide with anticipation. The two of them glanced at each other and laughed softly, like co-conspirators, then worked together to unfasten him.

The belt came loose, the zip undone, and a moment later Roland's cock sprang free — thick, hard, flushed with need.

Both women gasped, exchanging a quick whisper in their own tongue before looking up at him with mischievous smiles.

Anna wrapped her fingers around the shaft first, stroking slowly, deliberately, as if testing his weight. Then, without hesitation, she leaned forward and took him into her mouth. Her lips stretched around the head, tongue swirling as she sank down, her cheeks hollowing.

Roland groaned, his hand gripping the edge of the table for balance.

Click. Click. The camera, forgotten on its tripod, still snapped automatically on its timer, capturing the moment as Anna's head bobbed up and down.

After a few moments, she pulled away, saliva glistening on his cock. She laughed, wiped her lips, and gestured to Irena.

"Your turn."

Irena needed no convincing. She took him in eagerly, lips sliding down his length as Anna held the base steady. Her eyes fluttered closed, her tongue tracing him as she sucked hard, moaning faintly around his shaft.

Roland clenched his jaw, trying to keep control as both women knelt before him, taking turns, each hungrier than the last.

The hum of 14.6 filled the stable, wrapping them all in its invisible charge.

And Roland knew he didn't need to push the dial lower. Not yet.

This was enough. For now.

Roland braced himself against the table, watching the two women with a mix of disbelief and awe. Anna and Irena were no longer simply posing for his camera; they had slipped into something else entirely.

Their laughter came softer now, breathless, threaded with little gasps as they touched and teased one another. Anna cupped her friend's breast, her thumb brushing across the nipple until Irena shivered and leaned into her. Their movements were no longer for the camera, no longer self-conscious — they were swept along by the current thrumming invisibly through the stable.

Roland's breath came shallow, his body hot under his clothes, every nerve alive with the pulse of the field.

The two women turned to him at once, eyes glinting with mischief, with daring. They exchanged a few quick words in their own tongue — soft, conspiratorial, impossible for him to catch — and then both looked straight at him.

The air thickened.

Anna's smile widened, playful but unyielding, as though she and her friend had agreed on some silent challenge. Irena's gaze dipped lower, bold and unashamed, before flicking back up to meet his eyes.

Roland swallowed hard, the weight of their attention almost unbearable.

The laughter returned, bubbling between them, but it was different now — sultry, knowing. They were teasing him, delighting in his obvious arousal, delighting in their own boldness. Their hands never stopped moving, gliding over each other's bodies, squeezing, stroking, playful one moment, tender the next.

The machine hummed steadily on, and Roland felt the truth of it once again: this wasn't persuasion, wasn't performance. It was resonance.

Their natural barriers had melted. Their friendship had become touch, their touch had become play, and their play now hovered on the edge of something far more.

Roland's heart hammered in his chest. He had to remind himself — he was still in control. One flick of the dial, one quiet word, and he could guide the entire direction of what unfolded next.

And the two women, giggling, breathless, wanking and sucking his cock, glowing with heat, seemed more than ready to follow wherever the current carried them.

Roland's body trembled, the hum of the machine wrapping around him like a storm. The two women's mouths glistening with spit and juices— it all blurred together into one relentless current he could no longer hold back against.

His breath caught, his vision swam, and then the release came, tearing through him in waves so strong he almost staggered.

Anna and Irena cried out in delight, giggling as if they had won some delicious game. Their faces and lips gleamed with his cum, and rather than recoil, they seemed to revel in it —   continued sucking and milking every last drop, before turning back to him with mischievous smiles.

Roland leaned heavily on the table, gasping for breath, his chest heaving. The camera, still clicking dutifully every few seconds, captured it all: two radiant women glowing with laughter, and a man undone by them.

For a long moment, no one moved. Only the low thrum of the frequency filled the stable.

At last, Anna licked her lips and fingers and gave a wicked grin. "You are... very strong, Roland," she teased, nudging Irena.

Irena giggled, licking his cum from her fingers, eyes sparkling. "Mmm. Maybe too strong."

Roland tried to reply, but words failed him. He could only stare at the two of them — beautiful, daring, completely at ease with what had just happened — and realise that the machine had carried them all far beyond the boundary of a simple photo shoot.

And yet, as the laughter echoed in the charged air, he knew they'd enjoyed every second of it.

✦ ✦ ✦

Chapter Thirty One

Back in his bungalow, Roland felt the quiet almost jarring after the heat and laughter of the stable. He made himself tea, but it went cold on the counter while he sat at his desk, transferring the memory card to his laptop.

The screen filled with hundreds of frames, the shutter having clicked away relentlessly during the session. At first glance, it was chaos: blurred movements, half-cropped faces, the top of Irena's head, the corner of Anna's arm. He exhaled slowly, forcing himself not to be disappointed. This was always the risk with leaving the camera on a timer.

But he knew what he was looking for.

He started from the beginning, before the field had been switched on, before 14.6 had coloured their laughter and loosened their boundaries. There he found them — standing together, shoulders almost touching, giving the camera those first tentative smiles. The poses had been simple, a little stiff, but they were clear, flattering. Anna's hair fell perfectly over her shoulder in one frame; in another, Irena's smile lit her whole face.

Roland clicked carefully through, marking the ones worth keeping. He skipped past the later images, the ones where their play had tipped into something far beyond a conventional shoot. Those frames were his alone — proof of what the resonance could do, a private archive of the impossible.

For them, he would only send the safer ones. Enough to look professional, enough to keep their trust.

He copied fifteen photographs into a fresh folder, adjusted the brightness on a couple, cropped one slightly so the stable's rough beams didn't dominate the frame. Each adjustment was deliberate, precise, the movements of a man who now understood that presentation was as important as the session itself.

At last he attached them to an email, his message brisk and polite:

Anna, Irena — thank you again for today. Here are the first set of photos, as promised. It was a pleasure to work with you both. If you'd like more copies or adjustments, let me know.

His finger hovered for a moment before clicking **Send.**

The images would reach them soon — carefully chosen, innocent enough to share if they wished. But Roland knew that behind those frames lay an entire other set of moments they would never forget, even without a picture to remind them.

As the laptop hummed, he leaned back in his chair, a slow smile curling across his face. The machine hadn't failed him yet. And with every session, he was learning not just how to control it — but how to control himself.

Chapter Thirty Two

The week slid by in a haze of thought. The photos of Anna and Irena were already gone, sent and acknowledged with a short, polite thank-you. They hadn't written much more, but Roland wasn't concerned. Their laughter, the way they had leaned into each other, the teasing in their eyes, the touch of their hands around his cock, their mouths around his pulsing length— The look on their faces with his cum splattered across their cheeks, on their lips, in their mouths, none of that would fade so quickly.

But Emily was different.

She was the one who had asked for more. The one who wanted it again — and this time, filmed. That alone marked her as something beyond a passing experiment.

He opened his laptop, drafting a short note, weighing every word:

Emily,

Just a quick message to say I've been putting some thought into our next shoot. I'll have the right equipment ready so we can capture it properly on film. Everything will look professional — and discreet.

I'm looking forward to it.

R.

He hovered for a moment, then hit *Send*.

The stable would need a few changes before then. Better lighting, perhaps a soft drape to disguise the old beams. He made a list in his notebook: *new tripod, extra memory cards, a couple of plain sheets to act as backdrops.* Even a thicker rug to soften the cold floor and make the space feel less like a barn and more like a studio.

His hand tightened around the pen as he wrote. He could already picture it: Emily arriving, playful as before, stepping in front of his lens while the faint hum of the machine began to fill the air. And then, slowly, the change.

He shut the notebook and leaned back, his cock throbbing from the thought. This time, it wouldn't just be about what happened in the room. This time, he would capture it. Keep it. Replay it.

And that thought alone was almost as intoxicating as the session to come.

✦ ✦ ✦

Chapter Thirty Three

The reply came quicker than Roland expected.

Thursday evening works best. After six — I'll have the afternoon free. And yes… I'm still keen.

There was a single smiley face at the end, almost casual, but he knew better than to mistake it for anything innocent. His heart thudded as he read it twice, then three times, before clicking Reply.

Thursday, six o'clock is perfect. The space will be ready. I'll have everything set up — lights, backdrops, and the camera. You'll have nothing to worry about except enjoying yourself.

R.

Once it was sent, he sat back in his chair, his cock rising in anticipation already thrumming through him. This time wouldn't be a simple photo set. This time the lens would record everything — the shift from nervous laughter into heat, from play into something no one could fake.

The days crawled by, but Roland used the slowness well.

On Monday he drove to the stable with a boot full of supplies. A pair of freestanding lamps, their warm glow casting a soft circle of light against the rough stone. A thick rug, rolled out across the floor, softening the chill underfoot. A pale linen sheet pinned against the beams, transforming one corner into a studio backdrop.

On Tuesday he tested the camera again, attaching the tripod, adjusting the angle so it would capture both the backdrop and the rug. Then he tested the second camera — a smaller one, placed higher up on a ledge, pointing down, set to record continuously. This wasn't just about proof. It was about memory.

On Wednesday he cleaned everything again, wiping dust from the generator, checking the connections between the frequency unit and the two towers. He adjusted the dials with careful precision, fingers resting for just a moment too long on the one mark he had written so faintly he alone could see it: **3.3.**

By Thursday morning the stable had been transformed into a set — sparse, but purposeful, a place where something could happen and look entirely deliberate.

He walked slowly around the space, imagining her in it. Emily in her blouse, in her tight jeans, her camel toe, the first nervous smiles as she posed for the lens. Then the low hum beginning, the warmth creeping in, her body loosening. The moment she would cross into it her sexy playful way again, just as she had before.

And this time, he would have the live footage.

By late afternoon he was back at the bungalow, showered, freshly shaven, a clean shirt waiting on the chair. His stomach was tight with a mixture of nerves and hunger. Not hunger for food. Hunger for what her cunt. Hunger for what he knew was about to come.

When the clock showed five-thirty, Roland picked up his notebook, flicked to the last page, and wrote only three words.

Lights. Camera. 3.3.

✦ ✦ ✦

Chapter Thirty Four

Emily arrived just after six, her knock sharp against the stable door. Roland opened it quickly, forcing his expression into polite neutrality, though his chest was already tight with anticipation.

"Wow," she said, stepping inside. Her eyes roamed over the draped sheet, the lamps casting their golden glow, the rug soft underfoot. "You've really made it look like a studio."

"I told you I would," Roland replied smoothly. "This time it'll feel more polished. More… professional."

She smiled, nervous but bright. "Good. I've been looking forward to this all week."

At first, the shoot played out much as before. Emily stood before the backdrop, hands on her hips, her jumper loose but flattering. She posed with a soft smile, turned slightly to one side, then let her hair fall over her shoulder. Roland clicked the shutter, adjusted the lamp, gave her small directions. It all had the gentle rhythm of a real photoshoot, and Emily seemed reassured by the routine of it.

But Roland was watching more than just the lens. He was watching for the moment.

When she removed her jumper, revealing a white blouse that clung to her chest, he saw the shift in her body language — shoulders drawing back, chin tilting, her confidence beginning to flicker through. She looked down at herself with a little laugh. "You'll have to airbrush me," she teased.

"You look perfect," Roland murmured, meaning every word.

Emily's laugh lingered in the rafters as she stepped onto the rug, her jumper already folded neatly over a chair. The white blouse clung to her chest, every rise of breath pressing against the buttons. She moved with an energy Roland hadn't seen before — confident, eager, almost glowing.

The camera clicked, capturing her as she turned her hips slightly, one hand brushing her hair back, the other resting at her waist. Her jeans were tight, the seam pulling across her thighs. Roland swallowed hard, unable to stop his gaze from flicking lower, catching the sharp line of fabric where it pressed between her legs.

"Too plain?" she asked, glancing down at herself, then up again with a wicked little smile.

"Not at all," Roland murmured. "Stay just like that."

But she didn't.

She tugged at her blouse, slowly, deliberately, until the top two buttons slipped free. Pale skin gleamed in the lamplight, the edge of her bra exposed. The air between them thickened. Emily shifted her weight from foot to foot, her lips parting with the smallest sigh, as though even the simple act of standing there was becoming heavy with meaning.

That was when Roland turned the dial. **3.3.**

The hum filled the room, faint, almost imperceptible — but Emily reacted instantly. She drew in a sharp breath, her body swaying as if the floor had tilted beneath her. Her hands slid down her torso, fingertips grazing her stomach, lingering over the swell of her hips.

"Oh," she whispered, blinking, her voice low and breathy. "It feels... strange. Like I can't stand still."

"Then don't," Roland said quietly. "Let yourself move."

She did.

Emily arched her back, pushing her chest forward, then bent slowly at the waist, her hair falling like a curtain as she looked back at him over her shoulder. The blouse hung open now, her bra straining to contain the firm swell of her breasts. She laughed, a husky, breathless sound, and slid her hands down to her thighs.

Roland's camera clicked and clicked, but he could barely keep his focus. Every movement was alive with heat, every glance at him full of daring and hunger.

Her blouse fell completely open. She slipped the straps of her bra down her shoulders, teasing herself as much as him, until the cups loosened and she shrugged free. Her breasts were bared, nipples flushed and hard, rising and falling with her unsteady breaths. She cupped them in her hands, squeezing, pinching, moaning as though the sound had been pulled from deep inside her.

"God..." she murmured, tilting her head back. "I feel like I've wanted this forever."

Roland tightened his grip on the camera, forcing himself to stay rooted, to watch, to capture every second. His body screamed for release, but the power in restraint was its own intoxication.

Emily moved lower, unbuttoning her jeans with trembling fingers, pushing them down inch by inch until the dark triangle of her knickers showed through. The thin mesh left nothing hidden; he could see the dark curls beneath, the damp sheen clinging to the fabric. She pressed her palm hard against her cunt, moaning, eyes half-closed, and for a moment Roland thought she had forgotten the camera entirely.

The hum grew stronger, or maybe it was only in his chest. Emily gasped, swayed, then dropped to her knees, hair falling wild, breasts bouncing with the movement. She looked up at him through strands of hair, eyes dark, lips parted — and smiled.

"Tell me what you want me to do," she whispered.

Roland's pulse thundered. The machine had taken her past performance, past playfulness. She was raw need, desperate to be directed, desperate to give herself to the current thrumming through her.

And all he had to do was decide how far to take her.

Emily stayed on her knees, hair tumbling wild across her flushed face, her chest heaving. She looked up at him with eyes so dark they seemed almost unfamiliar — glazed with want, yet utterly focused on him.

"Please," she whispered. The word cracked at the edges, part plea, part command. "Tell me what to do."

Roland froze, his throat dry. He had known this moment would come, had imagined it, but the reality of it — her bare breasts rising and falling, the shine of damp fabric between her thighs, the machine humming like a low heartbeat through the room — was staggering.

Emily shifted closer on her knees, her hands pressed against her own thighs as though holding herself back. "I can't stop," she breathed. "I need you to tell me. Tell me how to touch myself."

The words sank into him like fire.

Roland steadied the camera in his hands, its red light blinking steadily, capturing every second. He inhaled, then exhaled, tasting the charged air. He could step forward, he could claim her — but the power was in this moment, in holding her there, in seeing how far she would go on his words alone.

"Emily," he said softly, his voice low but firm, "I want you to show me how badly you ache."

Her eyes fluttered shut as though the permission itself was enough to unravel her. She slid her palms over her stomach, down the swell of her hips, until they rested at the waistband of her knickers. Her fingers trembled, tugging the fabric taut, pressing against the damp patch darkening the mesh.

A sharp moan broke from her throat, raw and desperate.

"Yes," Roland murmured, the word slipping out unbidden. "Just like that. Don't hold back."

She obeyed instantly. Her hands cupped her cunt over the fabric, rubbing with shameless need, her breasts bouncing with each movement. She tilted her head back, mouth open, gasping, as though his voice alone guided her deeper.

"Take your time," he said, his voice slow, deliberate. "I want to see everything."

Her eyes opened just enough to meet his. A sly, aching smile crossed her face before she hooked her thumbs into the waistband and peeled the knickers down. The fabric clung for a moment, then slid free, baring her completely.

She spread her thighs wide on the rug, her fingers diving back between them with a shuddering cry. Her body rocked, her moans echoing against the stone walls, the hum of the generator pulsing beneath it all.

"Is this what you wanted?" she gasped, voice breaking as she buried two fingers inside her wet cunt , her whole body shaking. "Is this what you like seeing me do?"

Roland gripped the camera tighter, his chest pounding. He had never seen anything like it — a woman undone, begging not for his touch but for his guidance, her body moving in rhythm with the invisible current he alone controlled.

And it struck him then with piercing clarity: this wasn't simply about lust. This was power.

Emily's fingers moved with frantic urgency, in then out, her cunt spilling with wetness, her thighs trembling as she rocked against her own touch. Her moans filled the stable, rising and falling in time with the steady hum of the generator.

Her body shone under the lamplight — sweat slicking the curve of her back, glistening along her breats, damp tendrils of hair plastered to her flushed cheeks. She looked both ruined and radiant, caught in some raw rhythm that no pose, no performance, could ever have produced.

She opened her eyes briefly, locking onto Roland's, and the sound she made was half a sob, half a laugh. "I can't stop," she whispered, her voice hoarse. "I don't even want to stop."

Roland swallowed hard, his entire body tense. Every fibre of him screamed to step closer, to drop the camera and take her into his hands. But he held back, rooted by the knowledge that the power was in letting her destroy herself with need under his gaze.

"Good," he said softly, his voice rougher than he intended. "Show me how much you want it. Don't hide anything."

Her response was instant — her back arched, her head tipped back, her free hand clawing at her breast until her nipple stood swollen and red. She cried out, shaking, her hips rising to meet her own hand as though she were already being claimed.

Roland steadied the camera, capturing every frame. Her naked body, glistening with sweat, writhing on the rug, eyes glazed with lust. The pictures would be proof, but the reality before him was almost unbearable.

Emily gasped again, collapsing briefly forward onto her elbows, her hair falling wild around her face. She looked up at him from behind it, eyes wide, cunt wet. "Please," she begged, her voice breaking. "Tell me I'm yours. Tell me I can give you everything."

The words hit him like a physical blow. He tightened his grip on the camera, his knuckles white, his restraint stretched to breaking.

Her body shone, her moans rose higher, and Roland realised the truth of it: he could hold her here forever, begging, shaking, glistening with desire that only he could unlock — and the knowledge alone was almost as intoxicating as the act itself.

Emily's body tightened all at once, her thighs clenching, her back arching so hard her breasts thrust into the air. A guttural cry tore from her throat, two fingers, then three, then four fingers curling inside her wet cunt, raw and unrestrained, echoing off the stone walls.

Then it happened.

A sudden rush burst from her, hot cum squirting across the rug as she convulsed in wave after wave of release. Her hands scrabbled at her own skin, clutching her breast, curling inside her cunt, as though trying to hold onto the storm tearing through her.

Roland froze, the camera in his hand forgotten. He had seen women climax, but nothing like this — nothing so violent, so beautiful, so utterly beyond control. She was soaked, trembling, the rug beneath her darkened with proof of her surrender.

When her shudders finally eased, she collapsed forward onto her hands, gasping for breath, hair hanging wild. She turned her face upward toward him, strands sticking to her damp cheeks, her eyes glassy and desperate.

"Roland," she whispered, her voice hoarse and shaking. "I need more…I need your cock Please… don't just watch me."

She crawled toward him on trembling knees, her body shining with sweat, her breasts bouncing with each movement. Reaching out, she caught his wrist with surprising strength, clutching it as though it were a lifeline.

Her lips parted, trembling. "Please," she begged, her voice breaking with raw hunger. "I can't stop wanting you. I need your cock inside me."

The hum of the generator deepened in his ears, as though the machine itself were urging him on. For a moment he stood rooted, the full weight of the moment pressing down on him. This was the point of no return.

And Emily — flushed, wet, begging — was ready to be taken beyond anything she had ever imagined.

Emily didn't wait for permission. She was trembling, shining, still wet from her climax on the rug when her hands went to him. Fingers tugging, pulling, fumbling until she had him open.

Her eyes widened when she revealed his solid cock, and a ragged laugh escaped her lips — not of humour, but of disbelief at her own boldness. She curled her hand around his shaft, stroking slowly at first, then faster and faster, her gaze never leaving his.

"God, Roland," she whispered, breathless. "I can't stop… I need this, I need your cock."

Her lips descended, her mouth opened wide enveloping him with wet heat, moving over his cock with desperate rhythm. The sounds of her, the slick pull of her taking it in then out her mouth echoed in the stable louder than the hum of the machine. His hands tangled in her hair, and she groaned, grinding against him, taking in more and more, deeper and deeper, giving more, until she was rocking her own hips against the rug in helpless need.

The camera blinked its red light, recording every frame.

Roland's restraint snapped. He pulled her up to him, their mouths colliding in a hungry kiss. Emily clung to him, legs wrapping around his waist, bodies colliding with frantic need. They stumbled together onto the rug, clothing torn aside, skin slapping against skin as though the machine had stripped away the last threads of control.

Her cries filled the room, raw and desperate, being fucked hard and fast echoing against the old timber beams. His groans mixed with hers, each thrust met by a gasp, a plea for 'more, more… harder, harder' a moan that told him she was as lost as he was.

Roland was dimly aware of how wild it was, how reckless, how utterly consuming. But none of it mattered. The machine's low throb filled the air, and with Emily wrapped around him, begging to be fucked more, to be fucked harder, nothing else in the world existed.

When release came, it was violent, unstoppable, Roland pulling out just in time to spill his hot sticky cum across her tits, her cheeks, her lips tearing through them both like a storm. She clutched at him, squirted again and again, shaking, crying out his name as though it were the only word she had left.

The stable was silent after, except for the slowing beep of the camera and the harsh, uneven sound of their breathing.

The camera caught everything — the tangle of limbs, the sweat-shined bodies, cock in mouth, in cunt, her squirting, his cum over her tits, the blur of frenzied movement that went far beyond posing or play.

Emily pressed her face against his chest, hair damp and clinging, her voice muffled.
"Roland... take me again, now. I need more of your cock inside me. Roland's cock hadn't softened one bit, he looked into her eyes, she was pleading, begging again for more cock, more fucking, more of it all. 'That was something else.' She whispered, 'I want your cock in my cunt now'. Emily was insatiable, almost crazed with lust. Roland didn't need to hear any more, he flipped her onto her knees and lined up her ass, then gently, at first pressed the head to her hole and teased it, she started shouting out 'Yes yes, take me in my ass'. She backed up trying to force his cock inside but the hole was tight. Emily stroked her wet cunt lapping up the slickness and sliding it over his cock...then with one slick movement he was in her, slow at first, then deep, deeper, Emily moved her hips back and forth fucking his cock with her ass, clenching tightly. She wanted him to cum over her back, she wanted to watch it back later on her laptop.

The room was thick with sex, sweat, spill. Roland felt the rumbling of ejaculation build up again, he pulled back, his cock sprang out, then wrapped his hand around the shaft, wanking furiously, breath building up in his chest. 'Yes, yes, cum on me Roland'. His hand pumping in a blur as he moaned, hot cum spilled over her back, hot, sticky, dripping down her hips. His hand still pumping, cock still rock hard, hand pumping furiously as he came again. 'Jesus Christ…your balls are full' she cried out. They moved to the chair, Roland sat down, Emily straddled him, lowering herself to meet his hard cock, still yearning for her cunt. She lowered slowly, the slickness and heat brushing the tip. Then she slammed down, hard and forceful, spilling juices down his thighs. Hips bucking moving in rhythm, grinding his cock. 'Emily…I don't know how much longer I can….' She interrupted shouting, 'Keep going, keep fucking me, I want to watch this back at home. It is such a turn on'.

She was being fucked straddled, being fucked bent forward, being fucked bent backward, being fucked spread wide on her back, taking his cock in all directions in every position. Their moans echoing throughout the stable. The sound of juices lapping, bodies slapping together, raw, unashamed sex being filmed. Every grunt, every groan, every squirt, every hot spill, every second.

Until…..

Chapter Thirty Five
The Final Chapter

The camera's memory card was full long before they were finished. Its small red light had blinked until it could take no more, then faded to stillness, a silent witness that could not keep up with the bodies it was meant to capture.

The machine did not stop.

It throbbed on, its pitch low and endless, like some ancient chant reverberating through the bones of the stable. Each pulse pressed deeper into flesh, into nerve, into the place where hunger outstripped reason.

Roland had tried to pace himself at first. He had meant to guide her, to direct the scene, to remain in control. But the moment he turned the dial to 3.3, control was no longer his.

Emily had transformed in seconds — not playful, not teasing, but possessed. She rode him until she collapsed, then pulled him over her, urging him to take her again, and again, and again.

Their bodies became machines themselves, working past exhaustion, driven by the field's invisible hand. Sweat poured, muscles burned, lungs heaved for air that never came quickly enough.

And still they did not stop.

Roland had felt it in his chest — the pounding, the warning. His heart a drum beaten too fast. But her cries, her nails digging into his back, her thighs clamped around his hips — he could not pull away. He could not even think of stopping.

Emily's body shook with climax after climax until the pleasure became pain, and still she clung to him. Her voice broke into sobs of ecstasy, her throat raw, her nails leaving red welts on his skin. When her body gave out, she begged him to move her, bend her, take her in another way. She would not relent.

The machine fed them, drove them, demanded more.

Until the moment came when Roland's chest seized, when Emily's moans turned to a strangled gasp. Their bodies locked in one final spasm — the ultimate climax and collapse in the same breath.

They fell together, trembling, gasping, clawing at life that was already slipping. His hand closed on the rug, hers on his chest. Their eyes met once — glazed, desperate, wild — before the strength drained from both.

And then stillness.

Two bodies, lifeless, entwined, as though even death could not untangle what the field had bound.

The machine hummed on.

It did not care for their silence, their stillness, their end. It only filled the air, a constant invisible tide, as if it would go on forever, waiting for the next bodies to step into its reach.

Outside, the hedgerows whispered in the wind. Somewhere in the distance, a church bell tolled the hour. Life continued in the world beyond the stable.

But here, within these four walls, Roland and Emily had been consumed — not by each other, but by resonance.

The power he thought he could master had mastered them both.

And the machine waited.

Epilogue

It was three weeks before anyone thought to check the old stable. By then the door was swollen with damp, the windows clouded with dust, the air inside heavy with silence.

The police broke it open on a grey morning. What they found made even the youngest constable turn pale. Two bodies, collapsed together on a worn rug, skeletal with the passage of time but unmistakably entwined. Clothes torn, skin dried, faces slack with whatever final force had claimed them.

The machine sat in the corner, its twin towers leaning slightly, its generator dark and silent. The power had long since tripped. Whatever it had been doing.

The investigation spread quietly. They interviewed neighbours, acquaintances, anyone who might explain what Roland had been doing out there. His name surfaced in whispers, his odd retirement project, his supposed interest in "frequencies."

When they came to Sam's door, she listened in disbelief. Her neighbour, her friend. She remembered the cups of tea, the garden chats, his awkward but kind presence. Then she remembered the party with the machine, him wanking, looking out of his kitchen window.

Hearing how he had been found broke her.

When the detective mentioned the machine, she felt her stomach twist. She had known about it, yes — or thought she had. She had been told he sold it. She had believed him. Now the words came like stones in her chest.

"Did he ever talk to you about… settings?" the officer asked gently.

Sam shook her head at first, then stopped. Her throat tightened.
"What setting was it on?" she asked, barely able to breathe.

The officer glanced at his notes.
"3.3."

'Does that mean anything to you?' Sam shook her head then closed her eyes. A single tear slipped down her cheek.

The End

www.ingramcontent.com/pod-product-compliance
Lightning Source LLC
Chambersburg PA
CBHW060559190726
48283CB00003B/1079